His hair was slic
wore gray sweat
on his lean hips.
on the lounger opposite her, his legs caging Laila in, without touching her.

"I'm not sure if I should enjoy your refreshing honesty or search for a deeper motivation."

"Then why tie yourself to me in marriage?"

"Because my children will grow up with me." His dictatorial tone would have bothered her if she didn't see the resolve in his eyes.

"You're the last man I can imagine to happily settle into matrimony and domesticity and...our sons are not hobbies you pick up because you're in the mood to play father for a season."

"You claim to rely on cold, clear facts and not emotions, no?"

She nodded.

"From all the data you collected, you must already know that whatever my beliefs about you, and marriage, I would never let any harm or negligence come to any child, much less my own, *ne*? I will not let you cheat me out of what is mine."

The Powerful Skalas Twins

Taming Greece's most notorious brothers!

Billionaires Alexandros and Sebastian Skalas are known for the immense power they yield in Greece. But they'll be brought to their knees by the two women that can see past their ultra-rich reputations.

When the twin brothers are forced to swap places at the altar, Alexandros will step up as Annika Mackenzie's convenient groom while developing a very *inconvenient* attraction…

Read more in
Saying "I Do" to the Wrong Greek

Three years later, Sebastian still can't forget his night with Dr. Laila Jaafri. Once reunited, the consequences of their passion will force the playboy to do the unthinkable and claim her!

Read more in
Twins to Tame Him

Both available now!

Twins to Tame Him

TARA PAMMI

Recycling programs for this product may not exist in your area.

ISBN-13: 978-1-335-59352-8

Twins to Tame Him

For questions and comments about the quality of this book, please contact us at CustomerService@Harlequin.com.

Harlequin Enterprises ULC
22 Adelaide St. West, 41st Floor
Toronto, Ontario M5H 4E3, Canada
www.Harlequin.com

Printed in Lithuania

Tara Pammi can't remember a moment when she wasn't lost in a book—especially a romance, which was much more exciting than a mathematics textbook at school. Years later, Tara's wild imagination and love for the written word revealed what she really wanted to do. Now she pairs alpha males who think they know everything with strong women who knock that theory and them off their feet!

Books by Tara Pammi

Harlequin Presents

Returning for His Unknown Son

Billion-Dollar Fairy Tales

Marriage Bargain with Her Brazilian Boss
The Reason for His Wife's Return
An Innocent's Deal with the Devil

Born into Bollywood

Claiming His Bollywood Cinderella
The Surprise Bollywood Baby
The Secret She Kept in Bollywood

Signed, Sealed...Seduced

The Playboy's "I Do" Deal

The Powerful Skalas Twins

Saying "I Do" to the Wrong Greek

Visit the Author Profile page at Harlequin.com for more titles.

CHAPTER ONE

"MAYBE AFTER THREE years the shine is wearing off your marriage, Ani," Sebastian Skalas drawled from his seat at the brunch his sister-in-law, Annika Alexandros Skalas, had dragged him to that bright May afternoon with any number of threats.

Even the mention of that day three years ago when he'd disappeared on Ani because of *that woman* still made him angry. Luckily, it had ended up in forcing his brother to the altar. "It's not too late to dump Alexandros and come back to me."

Ani shook her head while his twin glared at him.

Her uncharacteristic quietness worried Sebastian. In the beginning stages of her pregnancy she should look radiantly happy. Instead, since he'd arrived at the Skalas villa near Corfu two days ago—upon her urgent request—she'd been withdrawn, irritable, even avoiding Sebastian. Which had never happened before.

They had been friends for years, as she had visited their estate every summer since she'd been an infant, as their grandmother Thea was her godmother.

He had assumed his twin had been overly concerned when he'd relayed Ani's request to see him—Xander was protective and possessive on steroids when it came to his wife. Now Sebastian realized Xander's worry was very much valid.

Since the three of them had sat down, Ani had watched the gates to their estate, looking excited and terrified in equal measures, every other second. And the fact that she had summoned, cajoled, threatened and begged him to be present for lunch for the last three days seemed like the signal for something big.

Suddenly, a car stumbled in through the electronic gates to the estate. Ani shot to her feet at an alarming pace that had both him and Xander rushing to theirs. As if the driver couldn't decide whether to go forward or backward, the car shot forward, then stalled and repeated the strange dance a few more times.

"Is it the baby?" Xander asked, a terrified look in his eyes that Sebastian had never seen before, and never wanted to see again.

Ani shook her head, grabbed Sebastian's hands, her eyes full of big, fat tears. A beat of dread pulsed through him, like he got before one of his migraines inevitably showed up. "What's wrong?"

Behind her, Alexandros looked thunderous. "What the hell did you do, Sebastian?"

Ani shook her head, half smiling, half crying. "No, Xander. It's not him…" She turned to Sebastian again, and threw her arms around his waist. "Just remember. I… I've been trying to do the right thing, okay? By all of you. I couldn't bear it if you…hate me for it."

Sebastian wrapped his arms around her trembling

form and met Xander's gaze over her head. His twin shrugged, looking as baffled and scared as Sebastian felt.

Ani pressed her forehead to his chest, soaking his shirt with her tears. "You've always been my first and true friend, Sebastian. Please, just… Just remember that I had to keep it from you."

"Ani, you're scaring me," Sebastian said, the sensation making his words sharp.

"This cannot be good for the baby or you, *agapi*. Calm down, please. Whatever it is, I'll make it right," Xander ordered in a gruff voice, his hands coming to land on Ani's shoulders.

Annika nodded.

Outside of their little tableau, Sebastian was aware of the little car finally reaching the courtyard. Heard the sound of the engine gunning, as if the driver wanted to turn the car around and run away. It sidled back and forth for a few more minutes, the tires digging grooves in the rain-drenched soil.

Irritated by the driver's hesitation, Sebastian caught his twin's gaze. "Are you expecting guests?"

Xander shook his head as Ani said, "I invited her here."

Finally, the driver opened the door and stepped out. Sebastian's nape prickled as he watched the woman. Instinct that had once helped him escape his father's brutal fists made Sebastian brace for some unknown.

Recognition hit him at first glance, a solid punch to his gut.

Tall and impossibly curvy, the woman was shabbily dressed in wrinkled pants and an oversize T-shirt, with thick, wild corkscrew curls. A high forehead and stubborn beak of a nose and a wide mouth, currently in shadows by the sun behind her, would follow. He'd have known the prideful tilt of her chin and the straight, aggressive set of her shoulders anywhere.

It was the woman he'd been searching for, for three years. Only today she wasn't all dressed up in a slinky red number, with her curly hair straightened into a waterfall, that mouth painted a lush red, the beautifully distinct amber eyes hidden behind brown contacts.

Memories came flooding back to Sebastian, suffusing his body with an instant heat. The silky swath of her skin that he had kissed and caressed with relish. The soft, sweet taste of her lips and how she'd clung to him after their kiss. The strange combination of open guilelessness and intense passion with which she'd begged for more of his words, his fingers, his caresses.

This was the woman he hadn't been able to forget for three years.

The woman who'd disappeared on him after an explosive night together, the woman who had stolen the one piece of leverage he had over their old chauffeur, Guido, who was the only person who had known where their mother had disappeared to two decades ago. He had been finally so close to finding her whereabouts, only for this woman to snatch away the opportunity from him.

What the hell was she doing here now?

He had no doubt that he didn't even know her real name.

Before he could ask Ani, she walked the few steps off the patio toward her guest. *Her guest...*

She must know this was his residence. And yet, she was here, willingly. Why?

Did she imagine he'd forgotten that she had stolen from him, that she had blackmailed him to stop him from coming after her? She'd been clever enough—no, brilliant, actually—to get one over him, and in staying under the radar for the next three years.

"Ani, what's going on? Why is that woman here?" He hated that he couldn't hide his urgency.

Xander stared at the approaching woman and then back at his wife, scowling. He cursed, finally picking up on the tension radiating from Sebastian. "Ani, *agapi*, what did you do?"

While she'd been near sobbing with Sebastian, Annika glared at her husband, her crotchety temper of late flaring. "I did what I had to do, Xander. I'd like to see you handle something like this. It's not always black-and-white, you know, and I'll thank you to consider—"

In a public display that still shocked Sebastian to this day, Xander pressed his mouth to her temple and said, "Breathe, *pethi mou*. I would never question your intentions."

Nearing them enough to hear the marital spat and the miraculous making up, the woman hesitated.

This close, the woman's amber eyes—intelligent and incisive—glinted like rare gems in the sunlight. As did the golden flecks in her hair. For all that she dressed without the minimum concern toward fashion or basic hygiene—there was an orange stain near her breast—there was that same vitality about her that had drawn Sebastian to her three years ago.

She was beautiful in a way a feral creature that stalked the woods was beautiful—without artifice, and with all her ragged, sharp edges intact. Even now, with anger thrumming through him, he noticed so much about her.

A tremulous smile wreathed Ani's lips. "Laila, welcome to our home."

Laila... Her name resonated through Sebastian like a gong.

The woman's smile came out a mix of a grimace and a baring of teeth.

Ani extended her hands, as if afraid *Laila* might be spooked enough to flee if she didn't tether her. "I'm so glad you came."

"I wasn't sure I would. Not until the last minute," Laila said, rubbing her belly in that nervous gesture he remembered so well. "I don't like decisions made on instinct, but..." She shrugged her shoulders, and with an implacable practicality he found fascinating, she straightened her spine and kissed Ani's cheek. "You're well? I have missed our chats."

"Yes. I've been ordered bed rest and haven't left the estate in three weeks." Ani's smile grew wider, genuine affection replacing her dark mood. "I've been so... eager for you to get here."

Alexandros threw him another glance before pulling a chair out for Annika. Sebastian did the same for Laila, who wouldn't quite meet his gaze and walked around the table, just to avoid being near him.

And yet, there was no doubt that her sudden appearance had everything to do with him and their encounter.

"This is Alexandros Skalas, my husband," Ani said.

Laila shook his twin's hand. For the first time since she'd walked up, a smile touched her lips. It felt like a slap to his face. Her body language was relaxed, easy around Xander, as if she were a porcupine that had retracted its prickles for the moment. "Ani said very few people can tell you apart, especially when you don't want them to know."

"Can you?" Alexandros asked, clearly digging.

Laila blushed and it was incongruous next to her serious expression. "Oh, I'd never mistake you for…him. You're serious and thoughtful and almost coldly logical, from what Ani tells me. Like me. Now, I can see it in the set of your mouth. Your brother, on the other hand, has a…" Then, looking thoroughly mortified at what she'd been about to say, she turned away.

"You know Sebastian, of course," Ani said, as if she couldn't let a moment's awkwardness land.

Laila finally met his gaze. Panic, nervousness and then a steely resolve flickered through hers, as if someone was changing channels to her emotions. "Hello, Sebastian."

The huskiness of her voice only made him angrier. "Come, Ani, finish the introductions," Sebastian said. "I'd like to know why it was so important that I meet your guest."

"You kept your promise," Laila said, looking shocked.

Ani floundered, then recovered, her cheeks a dark red. "Yes, well, this is Dr. Laila Jaafri, a statistics scientist. Laila got a PhD when she was twenty and has won so many awards in her field that it will take me the whole day to list them out."

"And why is she here, at our home?" Sebastian asked, rudely interrupting his sister-in-law.

"That's for Laila to tell you," Ani said, standing up.

For just a second, Laila's face crumpled, as if Ani was abandoning her at the cave's mouth to the big bad lion.

"I think your very brilliant friend is afraid of me, Ani," said Sebastian, watching her. "Maybe you should stay so that I don't gobble her up."

"It is ridiculous to assume that I'm afraid of you," Laila said, turning to face him, finally. "I'm simply unused to situations where I'm at a distinct disadvantage and there is no social precedent to follow."

"And yet you look like you're a second away from running."

"Sebastian, let her—"

He shot to his feet. It was extremely rare that he lost control of his temper, but the very sight of this woman made him feel unbalanced. "Clearly you're here to confront me, and yet you will hide behind my very pregnant and very kind and probably naive sister-in-law. Why do I feel like you befriended her knowing she's *my* brother's wife? What kind of a scam have you been pulling on Ani?" The more he gave voice to his suspicions, the more Sebastian knew he was right. "Alexandros, call security. Ani doesn't know that this woman is a thief and a cheat and—"

"Stop it!" Ani said, "Just give her a chance to—"

"You're upsetting her over me," Laila whispered, standing up so suddenly that her chair toppled over behind her. Then she poured a glass of water and brought it to Ani. Waited with a stubborn patience until Ani took the glass and drank several gulps from it.

Then Laila faced him, pulling a cloak of calm around her, even as he noted the erratic flutter of her pulse at her neck. "I came to tell you that 'our encounter' three years ago, where I seduced you, stole from you and blackmailed you, to protect an innocent man from your plans…" Her chin tilted up in a direct challenge, amber gaze pinning him to the spot "…had consequences… twin boys. I came here because I thought you had a right to know about them. To ask you if you wanted to be a part of their lives. And if you're not interested in that—" her shoulders straightened "—to ask that you contribute monetarily to their upbringing."

Consequences in the form of twin boys...his sons?

Sebastian's ears rang as if someone had set off a series of gongs near his head. He felt dizzy, disoriented, like he did during one of his migraines. He had two sons, with this woman who had approached him under false pretenses, slept with him and then stolen an important document from him.

Truth shone in her eyes, as real and bright as sunlight picking out the golden strands in her hair.

His emotions surrounded him in a dizzy whirl that he felt like he was in some kind of vortex. Like when his migraine medication didn't kick in fast enough and he needed to throw up. Like he was being battered from all sides and he couldn't escape fast enough.

Sons... He had two sons. Two-year-old boys. Twins, like Alexandros and him. Twins with a father who didn't know the first thing about being one and a mother who... had told him the truth two years too late.

He stared at her.

What kind of a mother was Dr. Laila Jaafri? What new trick was she playing on him this time?

Questions buzzed through him, but he refused to give them a voice. Refused to let her see how she'd shaken the very foundation of his life. Refused to let her see how thoroughly…inadequate he felt to meet this moment.

What are their names? How do they look? Were they rambunctious like he'd been or quiet like Alexandros? Did they get along with each other? Did they talk? Did two-year-olds talk?

More questions tumbled through him and his throat closed up in an instinctive, self-preservation response. All the conditioning he'd had in childhood and as a teenage boy came in handy because the last thing he wanted was to scare this woman off by showing his volatile emotions and his anger. He'd made a study of never losing his cool, of never letting anything matter to him so much that it touched his temper. It was the only way he'd known to survive his father's abusive rants and his meaty fists.

He turned away and his gaze fell on Ani. A jagged sliver appeared in his control. "How long?"

"Three months," Ani said, understanding his question, her face flushed with guilt.

Three months...

She had known for three months and hidden the truth from him. His one friend. His sister by everything but blood. He let her see how betrayed he felt, hardening himself against the flood of tears on her cheeks.

"Don't blame her," Laila said, taking a step in between them, as if she meant to protect his very pregnant sister-in-law from him.

Cristos, what did this woman think of him?

"If it wasn't for Annika persuading me that you..." She licked her lips, calling his attention to the beads of sweat dancing over her thick upper lip. "... I'd have taken longer to approach you."

"The better question is—" Sebastian rounded on her, some of his frustration leaching into his voice "—would you have told me the truth at all?"

"Yes."

"I don't believe you."

"I don't need you to believe me, nor do I have anything to prove to you, Sebastian. It has not been an easy decision to make."

"I don't believe that, either. I know how duplicitous you can be, Dr. Jaafri. How easy it is for you to spin lies, to fake interest, to get close with the intention of stealing from me."

"I did that because you were ruining an innocent man!" she burst out, her own temper finally breaking the surface. "And I never meant to sleep with you. It was..." Flaming-red streaks gilded her sharp cheeks and her mouth opened and closed like a fish out of water. "...unplanned."

"What a stroke to my masculinity that Dr. Laila Jaafri of the brilliant brain and the unending logic fell prey to my charms!" he bit out, sarcasm punctuating every word. "Since we're being honest finally, tell me, was it punishment for my sins that you would hide the truth from me?"

"Of course not. Would I like to have sailed through single parenting without a hitch and forgotten about the sperm donor who actively hates me because I stole from him to stop him from ruining an innocent man? *Yes!* Did I constantly, every minute of every day and all the sleepless nights, struggle with the fact that I was being unfair to my children *and* their father by not giving them a chance to know each other? *Yes!* Did I then gather copious amounts of data by stalking your friends and the woman I thought you cheated on the night before the wedding *with me*, looking for reassurances that you would not turn into a monster—as powerful men usually do when inconvenienced—who would take my children from me when I did tell you the truth? *Another resounding yes!* Did the fact that it is hard to raise two boys as a single woman with no parental or community support, financially and emotionally and physically, make it inevitable because I will not let my pride and misgivings about you become obstacles to the benefits my children will have with a father around? *OMG, we have another yes!*"

All of this she said softly, evenly, without inflection. And yet, the very lack of emotion in them convinced Sebastian of the truth.

"So you approached Ani with the intention of finding more about me? Where?"

"At the university where she takes music classes. After talking to her once, after she told me that your wedding to her would have been nothing but an arrangement between friends to help her out, I told her the truth." Her chest—delineated clearly even in the ugly, loose T-shirt—rose and fell, the only sign betraying the depth of her emotions.

And Sebastian realized one thing about Dr. Laila Jaafri. For all the games she'd played with him, she was logical. Maybe what she wanted from him…*was* what she'd outlined.

He looked away and his gaze clashed with Alexandros's. Like him, he looked stunned. So, Ani, as loyal to her new friend as Laila had been to the man she had been bent on rescuing, hadn't even told her husband.

As different as they were, in his twin's gaze, Sebastian found the answer he didn't want to admit.

Alexandros had spent his entire life trying to define who a Skalas man could be, *should be*, while Sebastian had tried to shrug off the oppressive expectations of the very name from the start. And yet, here was a crossroads he'd never thought he'd stand at.

This woman he didn't trust was the mother of his children. Whether he wanted them or not was irrelevant. Whether he wanted *her* in his life was irrelevant. Whether he felt equipped in any way to have a role in their life was also irrelevant. It was his reality now.

The Sebastian Skalas that had survived his father's abuse without losing his sense of self, the Sebastian that had dreamed of an affectionate, loving family as a young boy, the Sebastian that had spent years looking for a mother that had abandoned him and Alexandros to a monster she couldn't survive herself, would never turn his back on his…sons.

"Where are they?" he asked, in a surprisingly steady voice.

"With their nanny about two and a half hours from here," Laila said, probing his gaze. "Annika booked a luxury suite for us at this…posh hotel in Athens."

Two hours away...

At least Annika had the good sense to persuade this stubborn woman to stay at a good hotel and not some seedy hovel. He had a feeling that wouldn't have been an easy task.

"I thought you would want to see them," Laila continued, "As proof, if nothing else."

"Proof?"

"Proof that they are yours." Laila stared at his face in that clinical, academic way of hers, he realized now, and then at Alexandros. "They have your nose and that hair but my eyes. Of course, I understand that you'll do a paternity test."

He bristled at her matter-of-fact tone but managed to contain his irritation. "We will bring them here, now."

"I'd prefer to do it by myself." When he'd have protested, she hurried on. "They're two, Sebastian. While Nikos, older by three minutes, is friendly and trusting and very well-adjusted, Zayn is moody and sensitive. I can't just throw you in their faces. It will take…time. And I'd prefer to…"

"Nikos and Zayn," he repeated, feeling as if he was in a trance.

Instantly, they morphed from abstract two-year-olds to boys with real personalities.

Nikos was friendly and trusting and well-adjusted.

Zayn…was sensitive. Like Sebastian himself had been once and punished relentlessly for.

It was a miracle he could swallow, much less string words together. “My chauffeur will bring them all here.”

Laila shook her head. “It will be easier if I go—”

“You’re not going anywhere.” He opened his phone. “Which hotel?”

She studied him and then sighed. “They will be okay for a couple of hours more. We can discuss our… plans before we introduce them to you. I like to be prepared—”

“They’re my sons. Whether they understand it immediately or not, it’s irrefutable.”

“Yes, but I would like to know how involved you want to be. I have my own life and we’ll have to figure out sharing custody and other co-parenting—”

“Ah… Dr. Jaafri. Now I know you didn’t really pay attention to Annika.”

For the first time since she’d arrived, a flicker of confusion showed in her amber eyes. Sebastian lapped it up as if it were life-giving ambrosia. “What do you mean?”

“I will not be relegated to weekends and holidays.”

“It’s better if you chew on this before you make grand declarations. Parenthood is a one-way road with very little incentive in terms of excitement. It means giving up quality time for yourself.”

“So you think I should cancel my date tomorrow night with the hot lingerie model?”

She blinked owlishly. "No, you do not have to be celibate to raise your children well," she said, adding her own silken thrust knowingly or unknowingly, though he had a feeling that it was the latter, "but it demands some sacrifices. It's not my expectation that you upend your life."

Behind him, he heard Annika's sigh and Alexandros's choked outrage. "How very magnanimous of you, Dr. Jaafri. Why the change of heart after two years?" he said, biting down on the last words.

Hesitation danced across her face but she pushed it aside with the practicality he was coming to both like and abhor. "I would like financial assistance," she said, sticking out her index finger, as if she were highlighting bullet points. "Being a woman in an extremely competitive academic field with two little boys means I've already lost my edge, even before I returned from maternity leave." Out popped her middle finger to count out the next one. "I would also like some kind of reassurance that the boys will have a home in case I die suddenly." Third finger out now. "I would also like for them to have extended family. I grew up mostly fending for myself and it has dictated how I relate to people in general, although nature versus nurture is not completely out of the scope of our discussion. After meeting Annika and learning of your brother's strong family values and your grandmother's hand in raising you both, I felt reassured that Nikos and Zayn would benefit from being part of such a tight-knit family."

This time, the sound that escaped Ani was that of a wounded animal. If Sebastian hadn't had a father who'd tried his damnedest to break him as a boy with his incessant taunts and meaty fists, he might have made the same sound.

"Are you unwell, Annika?" Laila said, completely and clearly missing the nuance in Ani's response.

"She's dismayed at how, in all of your myriad considerations in coming to such an important decision," Sebastian drawled, "*I* seem to have very little role to play."

Fiery red streaks painted Laila's high cheekbones, and a soft "oh" escaped her mouth.

He didn't know whether to be relieved or horrified that he was a genuine oversight on her part.

"I will not lie to save your pride and say that you were a big consideration. Ani reassured me that you would never harm the boys or me, in any way. But not harming is not being a good parent."

"I know the distinction very well, Dr. Jaafri. And it's a good thing, no, that I don't give a damn about how much consideration you gave me in all this?"

"What do you mean?"

"I don't have to feel bad about railroading you into what I'm about to do. Even Ani couldn't have foreseen this, so don't blame her."

"Railroad me into what, Sebastian?"

"My sons will be legal Skalas heirs. Which means we'll have to get married."

"That's...unnecessary," she said, her amber eyes widening into large pools. A strange mixture of outrage and innocence shone from them. "You don't trust me and I...have no interest in marriage."

"Your wishes and dreams and plans don't matter anymore. Isn't that one of the first lessons you learn about being a parent?" He took a step toward her, gentling his voice. "I do not give a fuck about whether you intended to marry or if you have a loving fiancé back home, wherever that is. Only my sons matter now."

CHAPTER TWO

LAILA WALKED AROUND the enormous bedroom she'd been shown into, feeling untethered from her own life.

Sebastian had walked away after telling her he would *see* her when the boys arrived in an infinitely polite voice. If she hadn't seen and understood the scope and depth of his art, she'd have thought him the uncaring, ruthless, powerful man who had exploited an old man's weakness and driven him to losing his home.

But that night three years ago, she had not only stolen the promissory note he had taken from Guido as guarantee for his gambling debts, but had also gotten a glance at what Sebastian Skalas hid from the world.

The true core of the man he hid beneath his useless playboy persona. The profound beauty of his art had stolen her breath, pulled the very foundation of her assumptions about him, making her wish she'd met him under different circumstances.

But that kind of stupid wishing was not her. Neither had it stopped her from taking pictures of his art on her phone, to use as further guarantee that he would leave Guido alone. Even then, flushed with guilt and pleasure at sleeping with him, she had known that he wouldn't want the world to know who he truly was.

With that perspective that she had of him—that she knew no one else in the world did—Laila shouldn't be surprised by his easy acceptance. But she was.

Apparently, he believed her sons were his just like that, and it *was* a big deal that he had two sons. She'd expected, at least, garden-variety accusations thrown around about her character, her sexuality, her conduct and her tactics for gold-digging.

Instead, she'd been left standing in the middle of the patio, her stomach growling because she hadn't eaten anything since finishing Zayn's smushed toast hours ago, and the lingering feeling that he'd never forgive her. Which was strange because she didn't want his forgiveness in the first place.

Alexandros had pressed a quick kiss to Annika's temple and walked away, without meeting her eyes. Clearly, the Skalas men didn't abandon self-control even when they were angry. It was so reminiscent of her father that it soothed Laila, amid the gnawing confusion.

Her boys would have good male role models in their father and uncle at least. She added it to the positive column in her head, much like how Zayn collected his precious rocks.

Knowing she had a husband *and* brother-in-law feeling betrayed, Annika had looked as emotionally worn out as Laila had felt, and ordered the staff to show her to the guest suite.

So here she was at two in the afternoon, hungry and tired and sleep-deprived.

When was she not, to be honest?

Her brain glitched at the anticlimactic silence surrounding her. It wasn't just that she was away from the boys—she'd returned to work when they were three months old. Or that she had spent most of her adult life, and a good bit of her teenage life, looking after her father, then her mother and her sister and even Guido and his sister Paloma.

It was seeing Sebastian again. And knowing that all her preparation—stalking every piece of news and watching videos of him on social media in an unending loop—hadn't made an iota of difference to her reaction.

She'd had three years, and few enough moments without mom brain, to dwell on how decadently gorgeous he was. How his mobile mouth could mock even as his gray-eyed gaze stripped layers to see beneath. How he could be both entirely charming and exhilaratingly cunning with his quips. How some mysterious, magical thing she didn't understand had driven her to seek pleasure in his arms, bypassing all logic and rationale.

She'd thought she'd be…immune to his brand of physicality after all this time.

She wasn't and her brain didn't know what to do with this unforeseen glitch.

He was the most interesting man she'd ever met and three years and thousands of sleepless hours hadn't made a dent in her fascination with him.

He was still lean and yet somehow impossibly broad. There was a new sharpness to his gray gaze, a tightness around his mouth that she attributed to her arrival. He moved with a lazy grace and talked with an ease that she rarely saw in men who tried to dominate the people and situations around them.

No trying to intimidate the opponent for Sebastian Skalas. His power thrummed in the very air around him, making her prickly and aware. He'd tamped down his anger as easily as if he were closing his eyes.

Neither did she have any problem understanding his intent. He had meant it when he'd said, *"We'll get married."*

He meant for them to marry and live in this gigantic villa and play happy families for Nikos and Zayn. And she would be his plain, tall, big-boned wife burying her head in statistics, raising her boys in his gigantic home, feeling like a fish out of water while he…so beautiful that it hurt her eyes to look at him, went off to date stick-thin models, have sophisticated affairs, all the while laughing at her and the world. The very picture in her head made Laila want to run away and hide. Fortunately, the chirp of her phone pulled her out of the absurd reality of her marrying Sebastian.

The text was from the twins' nanny, Paloma, saying they were on their way and that the boys had settled into a nap. So, at least one stop to change their diapers and give the boys a minute—especially hyperactive Nikos—to stretch their chubby legs.

And she had three hours and one chance to convince Sebastian that his proposal was nothing but an invitation to disaster.

She found him swimming laps at the overhang pool out on one of the multiple terraces on the second floor, after walking the maze-like grounds around the silent villa, to the beach and back, and finally going up the open stairs that had a gorgeous view of the Ionian Sea.

The villa was built into the very side of the mountain, looking like it very much belonged there, with the Skalases reigning as undisputed kings. Of course, she had known he was wealthy, and in the last few months, she had come face-to-face with the fact that the Skalas family's wealth and power rivaled some of the richest people on the planet.

So what did a man like Sebastian Skalas—who had all this and the millions of euros that his paintings were in circulation for—need from an old chauffeur like Guido? So much that he had lured the old man into a gambling debt using his weakness against him, holding the threat of ruin on his head?

It was a question Laila had pondered for three years with no satisfying answer. And now, it came back to her again, given his easy acceptance of her claim. A missed step on the stairs brought her jarringly back to the world around her.

Her awe and admiration for the sea and the beaches and the near-floating palace that was the villa only lasted a few more seconds. Suddenly, all she could see were the dangerously open ledges and unending terraces and open stairs—a million places where her boys could get hurt.

When she reached the overhang pool on the second floor that seemed to stretch right out into the middle of the very ocean, though, she promptly forgot all her reservations.

Sunlight pierced through the bluest blue water and

painted the man's muscled limbs and smooth strokes with splashes of golden light. It would be better to approach him after he showered and dressed, give him some more time to cool down, although he hadn't really let his emotions show.

Despite the noise of her warnings, Laila simply went to him, feeling as if there was that hook under her belly button, tugging her toward him. Memories of sleek limbs and soft touches and hard nips… The one night she'd spent with him came back in a thrumming buzz, making her skin feel tight over her own muscles. A loose, lazy kind of heat thrashed through her and she tugged her T-shirt away from her breasts. The orange stain near her left boob—from when Zayn had thrown mango pulp at her—broke the spell and she came back to herself.

That night, that role she'd played to get his attention, had been a fantasy. Reality was that she was right now very hungry, and her rationale needed to be fed. She smiled as she noticed the covered lunch tray. Grabbing it, she opened the cover to find a colorful salad, pasta in thick white sauce and a slice of thick chocolate cake.

With an easy practicality that came with dealing with two prima divas all her life, and now two very energetic toddlers, Laila had learned to eat her food with gratitude and urgency. Also, it was a timely reminder that this would be her lot if she agreed to his ridiculous plan.

He would be out there living his usual, bored playboy life and she'd be left wondering where he was.

Not that it stopped her from groaning as the rich white sauce melted on her tongue. She attacked the cake next, her eyes going back in her head at the richness of the chocolate. The salad and sweet, tart lemonade were last.

If she wasn't aware of the sudden narrowing of Sebastian's gaze on her like a soft hum under her skin, she'd have spread her legs, unzipped her mom jeans, patted her belly and fallen into a much-needed nap before the boys arrived.

For a moment, she wondered if that was the best way to discourage him from his ridiculous proposal. Wasn't Mama forever telling her that no man liked a woman who ate like he did? Who was at least as smart as him if not more, and stood just as tall, argued logic all the time and made no effort to hide any of those obnoxious traits?

She ticked at least two boxes with most men and with Sebastian, she could also add the "men want their women to be at least as good-looking as themselves" rule Mama kept throwing in her face.

So maybe all she had to do was be herself.

After all, she was nothing like the woman who had taken on Sebastian Skalas. She was not beautiful—that routine with false lashes and hair straighteners and rented clothes had taken her two hours that evening—she was not a helpless damsel in distress and she was definitely not the wide-eyed, naive, out-for-a-good-time party girl she'd pretended to be.

If she was ruthlessly honest, though, he had thoroughly reduced her to the last part. Once she'd started chatting with him, she'd forgotten the whole reason she was there.

By the time he stepped out of the pool, she had a battle plan. Or so she'd thought.

Clad in black swimming trunks that outlined every inch of his chiseled body—taut buttocks and muscled thighs and a lean chest with a smattering of hair and bands of abdomen muscles—he made it impossible to not remember how that body had felt on top of hers. How much care he'd taken with her. How he'd taught her that she was meant for pleasure, too, and how he'd wrung every ounce of it out of her.

"I do not know if the hungry way your gaze travels my body is indicative of the fact that your defenses are down or if you've revived your act."

It was the last thing she expected him to refer to. And in that smooth-as-sin voice that wrapped itself like a warm tendril around her flesh.

Laila tilted her head back and licked her lips, feeling hunger of a different kind bloom in places she hadn't thought of in a while. Not since that night. "I have no energy left to put on an act. If you'd spent a little more time in the pool, you'd have found me snoring with my mouth open, drooling away."

"So you're eating me up with the same eagerness you showed the cake because you're lusting after me," he returned in such a reasonable voice that it took Laila a few seconds to process his taunt. "I feel like I have an upper hand for the first time since you appeared."

She blinked and looked away as he wiped himself. "I know you're not so starved for the female gaze to make this a scoring point between us."

"I'm not hearing a denial, Dr. Jaafri," he came back, lightning fast.

Laila would have docked him a point if he addressed her like that to mock her—she'd met enough people in life who used her brains as a weapon against her femininity—but he said it like it was his nod to her. "It's an exercise in exhaustion to deny things that are fact. Annika tried her best to do the right thing for all of us. I didn't tell you about the pregnancy or the boys all this while because I didn't know what you would do in retaliation for what I did to you first. And yes, I'm horny as any woman would be, especially since you're a super-stud on steroids and no, it's not a good thing or a bad thing between us." She sighed as his grin got wider. "Except it seems to stroke your ego as if you were a randy teenager in search of validation instead of a thirty-seven-year-old man."

"Now you sound like my grandmother Thea."

She didn't want to remind him of his grandmother. But maybe that was a good thing, too. "*Please*, will you put some clothes on? I can't think straight with all this…" She moved her arm in the air signaling at his torso.

Flashing another grin, he walked away.

Laila could breathe again and tried to take stock of the situation. Clearly, whatever shock he'd felt at her news had been handled. Because he believed her? Because it was that easy and of not much consequence to him? She groaned out loud. It was hard to remember she was dealing with a chameleon when he blinded her with that megawatt smile or that naughty twinkle in his gray eyes.

When Sebastian returned, his hair was slicked back, and he wore gray sweatpants that sat low on his lean hips. He sat down on the lounger opposite her, his legs caging her in, without touching her.

An invitation but never an imposition.

Sebastian Skalas toed that line so well.

"I'm not sure if I should enjoy your refreshing honesty or search for a deeper motivation."

"Then why tie yourself to me in marriage?" Laila probed.

"Because my children will grow up with me." His dictatorial tone would have bothered her if she didn't see the resolve in his eyes. "If you had come to me immediately after you discovered you were pregnant, I'd have demanded the same."

"You're the last man I can imagine to happily settle into matrimony and domesticity, and my sons…" Whatever fake warmth was there in his eyes turned to frost, and she backtracked. "Fine. *Our* sons are not hobbies you pick up because you're in the mood to play father for a season. They're a lifetime commitment and—"

"You claim to rely on cold, clear facts and not emotions, no?"

She nodded.

"From all the data you collected from Annika, you must already know that whatever my beliefs about you, and marriage and all those relationship traps, I would never let any harm or negligence come to any child, much less my own, *ne*? You're basing your character profile of me on nothing but vague impressions. So, no, I will not let you cheat me out of what is mine again."

There *had been* such warmth in Ani's words when she'd talked about Sebastian that Laila had found herself weaving fantasies about what it would be like to share her life and her sons with such a man.

Baba had been kind, fun, down-to-earth for a distinguished poet, and had showered her, and even her half sister, Nadia, when she'd allow it, with such unconditional love. After losing him, it was Guido, their housekeeper and papa's childhood friend, who had looked after her while her mother romanced man after unsuitable man, teaching Nadia to prize beauty and wealth and power over everything else.

Without Guido to hold her through the grief of losing her father, Laila might have unraveled completely.

"The picture I have of you is based on the fact that you'd have ruined an innocent man. You used his weakness for gambling to rob him of his home, the only thing he had, threatened him with ruin. All for what, Sebastian?" Laila said, glad for the reminder. "Guido wouldn't speak of what you wanted from him—"

"Where is *this innocent man* in all the hardships you faced?" he said, cutting her off. "Was he worth the elaborate farce? Was he worth sleeping with me?"

And there was the anger she'd expected, though only a small ember. Laila almost felt relieved at his silken thrust of a question. The deceit she had pulled on him had never sat well with her. Especially when he was the father of her sons. Especially when her entire life had been about taking care of others. Sometimes at the cost of her own well-being. That woman who had schemed to meet him, with the intention of getting close to him, the woman who had then lost all common sense and followed him to his apartment and slept with him… That was not her. Only desperation to somehow save Guido from his clutches and the genuine connection she had felt with him had driven her that far.

She hadn't realized until this moment how much she'd craved to explain her actions, how much she needed to hear his own reasons. "Guido died of a heart attack six months to the day after the boys were born. He was the first one to hold both of them. He spent hours on the floor playing with them. He stayed up with me so many nights when I couldn't get Zayn to settle down, when I'd have broken down and admitted defeat. The boys' nanny, Paloma, without whom I'd never made it through last year, is his sister. So, yes, the little I did for him, he paid it back a thousand times over, even before the boys, Sebastian. He was the one who watched out for me when I lost Baba, the one who held me steady through grief and pain. Nothing I did would have been enough to pay back the care he showed me and then my sons."

"It is your own fault that you had to depend on strangers." His polite mask slipped, and a hardness entered his tone. And yet, Laila had the strange, or delusional, notion that it wasn't directed at her. "Now, Nikos and Zayn will have my name and everything that comes with it."

"That's not possible if we share custody?" Laila asked, knowing that he had neatly sidestepped her question about why he had nearly ruined Guido. She wanted to push and prod until he answered. But right now, she needed him to back off this ridiculous wedding dictate even more.

"I'm not willing to share custody," he said without missing a beat. "You have admitted that it is hard to manage a career and the boys and all the financial responsibilities. I'm offering a solution that will satisfy both our individual requirements and…their well-being."

"So, I'd be free to devote myself to my career, with the added advantages this marriage would bring?" Laila said. Despite her best intentions, tendrils of curiosity swept through her. "If I were to be gone for days, or weeks, you would be present full-time for them? You would not use my career against how good of a mother I am?"

"Of course you would be free," he said, leaning forward. "There are a lifetime's benefits for you."

"Now you sound like an insurance salesman," she said, the very logic she trusted tasting like sawdust when it came out of his mouth.

This close, she could see the lines on his forehead, the thick sweep of his lashes and the lushness of his wide mouth. His very male presence and the heat it evoked in her and the logical offer he made—without a hint of anger or emotion peeking in—her own mind and body felt the cognitive dissonance. "A marriage like that becomes bitter. Nikos and Zayn will suffer."

"Not if we set clear expectations. What is that you truly want, Laila?" Her name on his lips, after all this time, made her feel dizzy.

"I've never dreamed of a partner or a husband or a

family or anything remotely traditional. Nikos and Zayn are blessings I didn't know I'd want. But that's as far as I can stretch my imagination."

"Why not?"

"Because those things happen to normal women. Not women like me."

He cursed and she flushed at how she was painting herself. She'd never been a victim before in her life, and she refused to be one in front of this man. She'd command respect in this relationship, if nothing else. "I'm stating facts, not looking for your sympathy. In fact, that expression in your eyes feels like an itch on my back I can't get to."

He laughed and it fanned tiny spiderweb-like crinkles around his eyes and his gorgeous mouth—a sign that he laughed a lot. At himself *and* at the world, in that sly, self-deprecating tone. That same quality pervaded his paintings, too.

"Maybe a husband would be handy with scratching that itch."

She pursed her mouth even as a smile wanted to blossom. He was disarming her one smile, one declaration, one question at a time, and they weren't even really for her.

"Unless the problem is that you already have a man in your life and theirs?" he probed, sounding so smooth that she almost missed the feral undertone to his words.

Laila stared, stunned at how he could change moods and masks.

"I will not play second fiddle to another man in their life."

"I don't have enough time to sleep or eat, much less romance some—"

"But you will have extra support now that you have come to me, *ne*? I don't think you comprehend how your life will change when it comes out that they are my sons and Skalas heirs. You have set something in motion you cannot control."

Laila leaned away from him, heart pounding loudly in her chest. "You're scaring me on purpose."

"No. I'm showing you reality as I see it coming. From staff you hire to long-standing colleagues, friends you've known forever to strangers you meet ahead, people will see you differently, want things from you, will take advantage of your elevated station in life. They will invade your privacy and the boys' hoping to sell the tiniest tidbit of their lives, your life, my life to some tawdry magazine. The only way to protect the boys from that is to protect you. To make sure no one takes advantage of you with the intention of getting to them or me."

"You don't have to clarify that it's all for the boys. There's no chance of me misunderstanding it," she said, sounding miserable and confused to her own ears.

Whatever he saw in hers, something gentled in his expression. "I believe that you didn't hide them from me with malicious intentions. That you came here today seeking very little for your own benefit."

Laila stared, stunned. For just a second, she wondered if he was manipulating her by giving her that. But he wasn't. Whatever his reasons, even with the past tangled in knots between them, he was willing to believe her reasons for showing up today and spilling a life-changing secret. It was more than she'd hoped for. "Thank you for that."

"Now, *you* have to see that I do not go around offering to marry women who hide big, life-changing things from me."

His words made perfect common sense, but Laila was afraid to go with her gut feeling, even when it made her feel good. Especially then. And something about Sebastian had always found a weakness in her.

"Tell me what would sweeten the deal," he added, leaving no doubt in her mind that he'd do anything to ensure Nikos and Zayn's future was tied to his.

"Nothing you offer could make me interested. I don't believe in love and marriage and…'all those relationship traps' for me," she said, using his own words.

"We're at an impasse, then," he said with a shrug, olive skin gleaming across taut shoulders, inviting her fingers for a touch. "The boys won't leave my side in the foreseeable future. And knowing the part you play in their lives, I'm loath to separate you from them, even for an afternoon."

If he'd said that in a threatening way, Laila would have sprouted thorns. But all she heard was his sense of loss at not knowing about them, his need to make it right. Was that the thing that drew her to him even now when she didn't truly know what kind of a man he was? Because she had seen that keen loss and that sense of purpose in another man's eyes?

"Baba…my father…" She cleared her throat. "He was a man who loved deep and true. I'm…sorry for depriving you of the boys until now. I only did what I thought was right for them."

His gray gaze held hers, a flash of emotions passing through, far too fast for her to catch any. For a second, Laila had the sense of standing at the edge of a cliff, looking into an abyss that promised untold delights if only you jumped. She wanted to run away with her sense of self intact just as much as she wanted to take a leaping dive.

Then his gaze flattened, leaving behind a touch of warmth. "You loved your father very much."

She nodded, feeling the loss deeply, even after all these years. "I did. Really, I've been fortunate…" She swallowed the sentimental words.

Even with all of Baba's love and care, she'd missed her mother. She'd desperately wanted to be part of her colorful life, wanted to drink in her exuberant personality, wanted to travel with her to all those fancy places that Nadia constantly teased her about. But that wouldn't be her sons' fate. "If you promise that Nikos and Zayn will have that… That's more than enough."

Sebastian's hand came up to tuck a curl behind her ear and every inch of Laila's body wanted to bow into the touch.

She shivered and swallowed, wondering how she was supposed to resist a man who could set her alight with one innocent touch, who was everything she shouldn't want and couldn't have. It was the same fight she had fought that night and lost.

The more time she'd spent with him, the more she'd realized there was more to Sebastian Skalas than the charming playboy or the ruthless predator of innocent men. So much so that she'd done the unthinkable and followed him to his bedroom and lost herself with him in a way she'd never done with a man, or even wanted to.

Now, again, he proved he was so much more even without answering her burning question. Even with the thorny knot of lies and half-truths between them, Laila felt that connection flare to life with one single touch, felt the need to give herself over into his hands. But there was so much more at stake between them now, more than just each other.

The worst part was that he was dangling himself in front of her, just within reach—a delicious, decadent prize, in some tragic parody of her deepest wish.

"Stay a few months here at the villa," he finally said. "Take as much time as you need to revive your career. Then you'll see that marrying me is giving the boys the best chance to thrive, with their parents together under one roof."

The need to ask his expectations if they married, to demand he promise her fidelity and more…hovered on her lips. Was it even possible after everything they had done to each other? Even now, he refused to tell her why he had targeted Guido in such a ruthless way. Even if he promised her the world and she accepted it, he'd soon tire of her. And she'd rather not face that inevitability.

"I agree, to stay here for a few months," Laila said, cautiously.

He leaned closer, temptation incarnate.

Laila dug her teeth into her lower lip to catch any wayward question and his gray eyes danced with a wicked light as if he knew how tempted she was.

"I hoped to provide some more data for your reassurances. But let's do this instead. How about I grant you three wishes, Laila?"

"Like my very own genie?" she said, unable to contain her excitement. She'd grown up living on those stories, hearing them in Baba's voice, always fervently wishing for the same one thing. "Except you're far too stud-like for any genie I ever imagined."

He laughed. It was a real laugh with deep grooves on the sides of his mouth and it tugged at her heart and somewhere else. "Yes, like that. Please feel free to rub me any which way you want. Though I will grant you three wishes without that, too."

She flushed and he grinned, the rogue. "You're a billionaire. A world-renowned artist, even if the entire world doesn't know it. You could probably charm the panties off a woman by smiling at her. Whatever I ask for, you can grant it to me easily."

"But there's the catch, Dr. Jaafri. I'm giving you a chance to up the stakes. You get to decide what you will ask me. But if I do grant you something…that truly makes you happy, that should count as a point in my favor, *ne*?"

"You can't…cheat your way through this, if that's what you're planning," she said, getting into the spirit of the challenge. It was a ridiculous bet, they both knew that. And yet, the spirit of playfulness beneath it had her arrested.

"I'm not the one who began our relationship on that note."

Laila sighed, knowing she deserved that. "So if you grant me three wishes that I truly want, I have to marry you," she said, laughing at the absurdity of the challenge. "If somehow you fail to grant me these three wishes, then you will agree to do this my way?"

He shrugged. "Yes. It is that simple."

Something about his confidence was heady and invigorating and so damned sexy. Something about the way he played with her, flirted with her, taunted her… was invigorating.

Laila wanted to bite that lower lip, and then kiss him. Only to find out if he truly wanted her, in this plain incarnation of hers. "Fine, I agree," she said, feeling a lightheartedness she hadn't known in years.

He walked away, leaving Laila feeling as if she was suspended upside down in a pool of honey, even as every inch of her thrummed with anticipation, with a new energy, just like last time. Except somehow it felt like, this time, he was the one casting the lure, and openly inviting her to walk into it.

And Laila was going to walk in with her eyes wide open.

CHAPTER THREE

SEBASTIAN HAD ASSUMED he was prepared—mentally and emotionally—by the time the chauffeur-driven car pulled into the courtyard, as close as it could get to the wide steps, where he and Laila were waiting. But his heart—lodged in his throat—made it impossible to lie to himself.

He was excited and terrified in equal measures. For a man who'd fought so hard to not be molded into a template of his perfect twin, he found himself wishing Ani and Alexandros hadn't given him privacy to face his sons for the first time.

As some sort of buffer to guard *them* from him—what if he reacted wrong? What if, like all the times Konstantin had mocked and torn into him, something was wrong with him? What if he felt nothing for these two innocent children that were his responsibility?

The what-ifs were endless, but fear was not new to him, and Sebastian refused to let it cow him now when he hadn't let it when he had been a powerless, innocent child.

He wrapped his hand around Laila's wrist, right at the moment when she'd have flown off the steps to meet them, to anchor himself rather than to stop her. An instinctive weakness he couldn't hide.

Her entire body stilled, and her head tilted down to look at his fingers. Then, as if they'd done this very ritual countless times, she laced her fingers around his. Her fingers were soft against his but there was also strength in them.

Without turning to look at him, she said, "For almost a month, after they were born, I was terrified every time I had to hold them. It's normal."

He simply nodded, unable to parse his feelings, wondering at how easily she offered reassurance when she had had none for the very same situation. Or rather, she'd had support, in the form of the very old man he'd been intent on destroying.

A woman, in her sixties, was the first one to step out of the car. She bent and time seemed to move inexorably slow as she plucked out a boy from the car and set him on his feet.

Smiling and stooped, she held his shoulders as his fat legs in shorts stumbled for a second like a newborn calf. Then, with a sudden whoop at the sight of his mother, he shrugged the nanny's hands off and ran full steam toward Laila.

From the wide smile and eager, inane chatter he kept spewing, Sebastian realized this was Nikos. His firstborn. His easy, affectionate, well-adjusted son.

Laila had been right about their physical resemblance, too—his son had the jet-black hair and the sharp nose of the Skalas family. But his eyes were like his mother's—a warm amber that practically glowed and changed the very landscape of the toddler's face, as if in defiance of the mighty Skalas genes that his father had been so proud of.

When Laila folded her legs to sit on the lowest step so that she was face-to-face with Nikos, Sebastian followed suit gladly, his legs nearly folding under him like they were made of matchsticks. He felt hollowed out with fear and something more, as if his insides were held together by strings outside his own body, as if this little boy or his brother could pull them as if he were a puppet and Sebastian would move and act as they bid him to.

Nikos reached them with eager cheer and easy smiles and wrapped his arms around his Mama's knees. For all his exuberant personality, it was his tiny size that struck Sebastian like a fist to his chest.

"Mama, Mama…on the way, I see horsey. Can I pet? Can I ride? Please, Mama. I be good boy for Granny."

Laila pressed her mouth to his temple and laughed, her hands moving over his tiny frame. The sound was full of such pure, incandescent love that it sounded alien to his ears. Sebastian had to swallow so that the strange, husky cadence of it didn't cling to his throat.

"Hmm… We'll have to make sure it's safe first, yeah, baby?" Laila said, running her fingers through his wind-ruffled hair. "Because horses are big and wild."

Dutifully, Nikos nodded. "Safe, yeah." Then he pinned those amber eyes on Sebastian, quite like how his mother had done that very morning, and Sebastian thought something he hadn't known inside him had been cracked open, never to be patched up or closed again. Like a vast abyss full of prickly things like vulnerability and joy and love and pain. An abyss that seemed to spring out of himself, one he'd avoided looking into for so long.

A gap-toothed grin appeared as Nikos said, "Hi."

Sebastian croaked out a "Hello, Nikos," as if he was the one who didn't know how to form words yet.

"You know horsey?"

Sebastian laughed. The sound seemed to come thrashing out from below his chest, through his diaphragm in an action his body was unaware it could perform until now. "Yes, Nikos. I might know horsey."

His good cheer growing, Nikos turned to his mother. "Friend, Mama? Not stranger?"

Hands squeezing Nikos's shoulders compulsively enough that the little boy bristled against his mother's hold, Laila trembled. But she met Sebastian's gaze over his head, ever the brave one. Then she gathered Nikos closer to her chest, kissed his temple again, before she said, "Nikos, this is your papa."

"Papa? My papa?"

Laila nodded, tears spilling out from her eyes.

"Hi, Papa," Nikos said, as if this was as easy and understandable as the sky was blue and the horse was big and then he made a jump from his mother's lap toward Sebastian that probably took a decade off Sebastian's life span.

Shaken to his core, he caught the little body. The scent of baby powder and dust and bananas hit Sebastian as he gathered his son to himself, his hands shaking, his breath a hurried whistle, terrified that he might do something that would spook the small boy.

But Nikos was as courageous as Sebastian himself had been once. Utterly unabashed, he threw his arms around Sebastian's neck and said, "Hi, Papa." His heart thundered like a drumbeat as he took in the stubby nose with crust under it and the wide amber eyes and the thick lashes. Now his heart felt like it was being squeezed in a vise, and that, too, was an ache he hadn't known in such a long time that it was now unfamiliar.

Nikos looked up into Sebastian's face, one grubby finger tracing his cheekbone, and said, "You take me to horsey?"

And Sebastian was laughing again, but there were tears in his eyes, too, and it was another thing he didn't know he was capable of—to laugh and cry at the same time—and he didn't care if Laila saw them. He sniffed like a baby, pressed a kiss to his son's head and said, "Yes, Nikos. Papa take you to horsey."

In response to Nikos's loud cheers, Laila groaned and laughed and told Sebastian in quite the stern voice that their sons would never learn to speak properly if she and Sebastian didn't speak in complete sentences to them, and Sebastian told her his son spoke perfectly enough for him and to hell with the entire damned world. And in the secret chamber of his heart that had frozen to ice a long time ago, he felt a crack. It felt good to belong to something bigger than himself, something purer than what the Skalas name and family had stood for, something that had this woman looking at him with a strange mixture of reluctant trust and utter openness.

* * *

His meeting with his second son was as much an emotional roller coaster as meeting Nikos but more…heart-wrenching, as if he'd been suspended at the scariest part of the ride, to hang upside down, his heart threatening to beat out of his chest.

And that's how it would be from now on, Sebastian realized. The stupid organ that he had no use for until now was to be wrenched and shaken and played around this way and that by these two little boys.

A few minutes later, Laila had spread a thick blanket right on the acres of perfectly manicured lawn for an impromptu picnic, claiming she wanted to give the boys time to run around after their nap and before bringing them inside to new surroundings. Nikos was drinking water from his bottle, eating crackers she handed him and casting glances at and asking numerous questions of Sebastian—mostly about what the horsey ate and did and played with—when the old nanny brought Zayn, who'd been napping longer, out of the car.

He didn't run toward Laila like Nikos did. In fact, he seemed to be against the very idea of coming close to his mama, as long as she was sitting near Sebastian.

With a softly murmured, "Please give him space," and a tremor she couldn't hide, Laila got up from the blanket and started chasing Nikos across the green lawn, all the while keeping an eye on Zayn and chatting to him about the car ride and his nap.

Sebastian, feeling as if he'd been ordered to sit out his favorite game—which had been an actual punishment Konstantin had meted out to him more than once—took himself off the blanket, hoping Zayn would understand that he posed no threat.

Finally, after a few minutes of watching his mother and twin, a tiny notepad and pencil clutched in his tiny hands as if they were his precious possessions, Zayn approached his mother and hugged her legs. Immediately, Nikos grabbed his hand and dragged his younger brother forward. “Zayn, this Papa. He show horsey to us. You wanna come?”

While his twin’s reassurance was enough to join in on the play and to hug his mother in this new, strange location, it didn’t seem to hit the mark for Zayn when it came to trusting Sebastian. He took a step back to hide behind his twin’s body, his amber eyes far too intensely focused on Sebastian’s face for a two-year-old boy.

“Papa, Mama?” he said, after a long while, having heard his twin bandy about the word with a ferocious sort of pleasure.

Laila nodded, opened her mouth—no doubt to urge him to greet Sebastian—and then decided against it.

Zayn gave a grave nod in return, as if agreeing to process this new material, but promising no more, and then completely avoided Sebastian.

Like a laser pointer creating heat on his skin, he could feel Zayn’s gaze on him from time to time, but the moment he tried to make eye contact, the little boy looked away. Which meant Nikos stayed away, too, because clearly, his first loyalty was to his twin.

Just as Alexandros’s loyalty had been to Sebastian, all those years ago, enough to take on the impossibly powerful Konstantin, even as he threatened Xander’s ruin for that loyalty. Sebastian looked away, the past and the future blurring in front of his eyes and in his head. He pressed his fingers into his temples, feeling the shadow of an ache there.

That won't be necessary with his boys, he vowed to himself. Nikos wouldn't have to shield Zayn from anything, much less their own father, because Sebastian would do it for both of them.

While every inch of him urged him to gather Zayn in his arms and cocoon his sensitive son from the very world Itself, Sebastian fought the overpowering instinct. They were both here now, and he felt as if he had been swimming under water for too long, and he would not do a single thing that would upset his sons. He would not be his father, turning everything into ego, twisting what it meant to be a man, claiming they had to act a certain way to be worthy of the Skalas name.

He would not let his sons down. He would not let Laila down.

Suddenly, all the distrust he'd thrown in her face seemed like dust motes amid gratitude for how bravely she'd brought them into his life.

For years after she'd abandoned them to Konstantin's mercy, Sebastian had wondered where his mother had disappeared to, how she had fared, wondered if she'd thought of him and Xander, wondered if she was well. All he had known was that Guido, who'd worked as their chauffeur for one summer, had helped her escape, had been the only man who had known her whereabouts.

It had taken him years to track down the old chauffeur, a little more to understand his weakness for gambling, then he'd taken his house from him, knowing that shame, if nothing else, would persuade the old man to spill Sebastian's mother's whereabouts. He'd been desperate to find his mother as a young teen, but as a grown man, it had become an obsession, in the absence of any real purpose.

In pursuit of that piece of truth from his past, he'd threatened ruin for Guido, the very man who had helped Laila take care of his sons. Until now, that man had been only a step in his pursuit, an obstacle in his goal. But now, thanks to Laila, he couldn't unsee Guido as a kind old man who had once cradled his sons in his arms with tender care.

Guilt gnawed at Sebastian's insides. Having heard the affection in her voice when she spoke of Guido now, he understood that she'd done whatever needed to protect a loved one. Just as he or Alexandros would have done.

And she also had every reason to think the worst of him and to stay away.

She loved his sons like no one else would—not even himself maybe—and she'd tangled with him to protect a man who had been kind to her. Now, she'd taken a chance on Sebastian, despite what she called calculating the odds.

It was his turn to show her that trust, to win her over, to give her everything she'd ever wanted in life for the gift she'd given him. To prove to her that she and the boys belonged with him.

Any momentary hesitation he'd felt about having two little boys to care for, to nurture and protect, dissipated, leaving behind a crystal-clear clarity he had never known in his life.

He had already fallen in love with his sons. It was a deluge, this sudden gripping, intense need to protect them, and hold them close and to have them near for every sweet and hard moment, a primal urge to walk into the now quiet bedroom where they were resting and watch over them for the rest of the dark nights and sunny days, a profound, gut-wrenching kind of relief to know he could feel so much for them, that Konstantin hadn't beaten that particular ability out of him.

Sebastian rubbed a hand over his face, shaking and shivering under the onslaught of emotions.

This was what he'd needed in his life, even if he hadn't known it until now. For the first time in his adult life, he wasn't simply meandering through it, trying his best to detach from the Skalas name and empire, burying himself in his art, wasting himself away on shallow experiences that drained his mind and body.

Now, he wanted his life to take a certain shape and he would actively pursue it.

Whatever instinct had propelled him to demand Laila marry him… It carried the weight of his deepest, most secret desire within it.

For his sons to be happy and well-adjusted and thriving, they needed their mother and he needed them in his life. Ergo, his primary goal now was to do anything to keep Laila in his life.

And while he'd have never admitted openly to his brute of a father, Sebastian had always known he could be just as ruthless as Alexandros, for all that he wore different masks for the world. He simply hadn't cared about anything enough, except finding his mother.

While his twin had devoted his ruthless will to ousting their father and rebuilding what it meant to be a Skalas man running the prestigious bank, Sebastian's own willpower had never been interested in anything. Until now.

He was keeping his sons and he was keeping their mother in his life, even if it meant he had to seduce every inch of logic and rationale out of Dr. Jaafri. And he would make sure she not only enjoyed the seduction but that she had everything she'd ever wanted in her life. He would make all her wishes and dreams come true. It was only a matter of getting her to admit them.

For himself, there was nothing he enjoyed more than a challenge with high stakes. Despite her lies and her one attempt at blackmailing him—all to protect Guido—he hadn't stopped thinking of her for a single day since she'd disappeared. So, it wasn't as if it was a hardship to seduce her.

As it was usually with him, she'd become an obsession, not just because she'd left him wanting more, but also because she'd gotten the closest to the one thing he held sacred in his life—his art. Now to know that she'd done it all to save a man he'd been bent on ruining…just for a piece of information that would unlock his own past. To reach a woman who'd abandoned him and Xander years ago.

Cristos, even for him, it was twisted.

But now that she was back in his life, with a gift unlike he'd ever received and not even known he needed, he would fix it all.

CHAPTER FOUR

IT SHOULD HAVE felt strange to have Sebastian shadow her and the boys for the evening. Laila had found it nerve-racking when Mama and Nadia had visited a month after the boys had been born. And then when the boys had turned one.

Mama had criticized her about everything—that Laila was sharing the bed on alternate nights with Nikos and Zayn, that she didn't impose enough structure on them or that they had too much playtime or that she let them eat from her plate.

It had taken all her goodwill to not point out Mama's own flaws and faults in how she'd raised Nadia. For Laila, it was Baba who'd taken care of everything.

First, she hadn't even expected him to show up. She had compulsively followed enough of his wild, playboy exploits to know that he was a man who was bored easily, who thrived on unconventional risks, who chased every high like his life depended on it. And really, on their best day, her boys were exhausting and demanding. So, she'd been shocked when he'd arrived to get them ready for sleep.

When she got over that initial shock that he actually

wanted to be part of their actual routines and rhythms, she'd braced herself to be watched under a microscope, to be weighed and judged and criticized. To be questioned.

He turned her assumptions upside down, yet again. The man had possessed a knack for making Laila feel good in her own skin in just a few hours. He'd made her laugh, step out of herself for a night. Now, she had none of that polish and fake sophistication, and yet, that same sense of ease lingered with the warm, easy energy he put out.

Through playtime and dinner and bath time and story time, he had been a quiet, easy presence in the background, keeping up a soft, slow dialogue with all three of them, without quite crossing the invisible boundary that Zayn had drawn.

It helped that Nikos, as ever, kept up their little unit's momentum, demanding to play, to eat, to be read to, on schedule and that he gave Sebastian one-word answers even as Zayn quietly observed them. By the time they'd settled into bed, Nikos had extracted another promise about the horsey from his papa.

Laila went to shower, leaving Sebastian standing outside the vast bedroom that had magically been arranged with two cribs, a changing table, a number of stuffed animals and toys in shiny new packages, and any number of paraphernalia that the boys could need, in just a matter of a few hours. Without Laila even broaching the topic, he had arranged for Ani and Alexandros to move to the second floor since the numerous open terraces and stairs were dangerous for the boys.

Being a caregiver apparently came easy to Sebastian Skalas, as easily as stunning art and that wicked, sinful smile. As hot water pounded through her tired muscles, Laila couldn't help but wonder if being a good husband would come easily to him, too.

Having dressed in an old T-shirt and a pair of shorts that suddenly felt too tight across her butt, Laila arrived in the attached bedroom to find Sebastian standing on steps that led directly to a private strip of beach from their suite.

With the moon full and high in the sky, silvery light danced on his hair, delineating the breadth of his shoulders and the taper to his waist. He was simply dressed in a linen gray shirt and black trousers and yet, somehow, he managed to highlight the powerful masculinity that seemed to thrum around him.

Laila felt tired to her bones. It had been an especially trying day, and she should have crawled into bed and let exhaustion take over. While Paloma would be the first one to wake usually if one of the boys was up during the night, Laila had given her tonight off. It was a new, strange place and she wanted to be the one they saw if they woke up feeling disoriented. Or maybe it was she who needed the comfort of snuggling one of them in her bed, since she felt more out of element than either of them. Even Zayn, while his usual reserved self, had been constantly taking everything in with those wide eyes.

The loneliness she'd endured for so long came back with a sudden bite, keener and sharper now. As if something inside her knew that what she'd wanted all along was within touching distance. Which was strange, because as she'd told him, Laila had never entertained ideas of romance or marriage. After giving birth to twins, it had become even more distant, for no man wanted to raise another man's twins. Not that she'd even considered the option of dating or fun or anything that didn't remotely concern her sons and her career and how to juggle it all.

But something about Sebastian had always called to Laila. She'd crossed so many of her self-laid boundaries back then and apparently that draw he had held for her hadn't dimmed one bit.

It was simple curiosity, she told herself, basic need for adult company, since she spent every waking hour—and some half-asleep ones—deep in dialogue with two toddlers or in statistics models she hadn't yet solved.

The stability and complexity she had sought in her career all her life suddenly didn't seem enough. Apparently, her body equated Sebastian Skalas with risk and how well and pleasurably it had paid off last time. Awareness didn't make her immune to Pavlovian responses.

She gave in to the urge and reached the cozy landing off the bedroom where he stood. Two bowls sat on the coffee table, one full of fruit and the other covered. Lifting the lid on the second, she found thick creamy yogurt with an assortment of nuts and seeds and honey in smaller bowls around it. He'd remembered the snack she'd asked for the first time they'd woken up tangled in each other that night. Warmth flickered in her chest, even as she reminded herself that the second time, she'd woken up alone and had gone through his apartment.

"Thank you for making today easy," she said, conveniently to his back. To avoid meeting his eyes, she busied herself with adding the nuts and seeds to the yogurt, and then a generous dollop of honey on top. She licked one thick streak from her thumb, and looked up to find his gaze on her mouth.

Heat licked through her blood, like the very honey on her tongue. Suddenly, she was aware of the heavy achiness of her breasts, and a loose, languid pulse fluttering low in her belly, right at the center of her core, desperate for friction.

"Is there anything else you need for tonight?" he said in such a matter-of-fact voice that Laila instantly felt foolish. It was all in her head, then—the lick of heat she'd seen in his eyes.

"No," she said, tugging the ends of the threadbare oversize cardigan she'd thrown on at the last minute over her worn-out T-shirt. "You thought of everything."

He nodded and then took the seat opposite hers, while she stirred the honey in.

A soft briny breeze was a welcome relief against her overheated skin while the yogurt was thick and creamy against her tongue. The quiet, breathtaking beauty of the setting, the sudden silence after hours of constant chatter from Nikos and Zayn, seemed to amplify the tension she felt around him. Spending too much one-on-one time with him was a bad idea, her gut said, and for once, she knew she needed to heed the instinctual voice.

"Am I speaking out of undeserving paternal pride,"

Sebastian said, stretching his legs, his fingers steepled on his abdomen, "or are they especially easygoing for two-year-old boys?"

Laila smiled at the lingering awe in his voice. It was good to know he was capable of those emotions, at least for their sons, and felt no shame in expressing it. "They *are* easygoing. Your paternal pride, I'd say, is not undeserving, either. You have a knack with children. Annika..." she said, hesitant to bring up the other woman but wanting to make sure he understood she'd only done the right thing, "told me you used to spend endless hours playing with her."

He shrugged, his gaze on the ocean. In profile, in repose, the magnetic quality of his presence should have been minimized, at least blunted. And yet, there was still that near-violent thrum around him, as if he was forcing himself into stillness and calm.

"Alexandros was too busy studying, doing magic with numbers and trying his damnedest to please Konstantin, to indulge in silly games with me. Ani...made it easy to escape the things I loathed. Which was everything, living under my father's thumb. Entertaining myself while I watched her for Thea and played with her...was purely selfish. It also had the added benefit of getting under Alexandros's skin, because even back then, he cared about her more than he would ever let on."

Laila absorbed every word and nuance like a sponge parched for water. There was such fondness when he talked of Annika and yet, he had refused to even look at her again after Laila's arrival. Something about how he framed it made her frown. "Is there a selfish motive in how you behaved with the boys today, then?"

He smiled. And it was the soft, disarming smile of a predator, who for some reason wanted her to feel safe with him. "Of course there is. I want them to feel safe with me, to trust me. To let me in. I know Nikos warmed to me pretty quickly, but I didn't miss how much Zayn's behavior dictates his own."

"You don't miss anything," she said, feeling both relief and a strange dread at the realization.

"You fooled me very thoroughly that night," he quipped, one corner of his mouth tugged up. The lack of any rancor only made her want to explain.

"I didn't mean to. Or I mean, yes, I meant to corner you and demand some kind of…answer for why you were targeting Guido. I dressed up so out of my comfort zone, spent hours making myself up because you would've never paid me attention in my usual getup," she said, pulling at her T-shirt. "But everything that happened after I actually met you, that was unplanned. It spiraled into…something else. I didn't plan to sleep with you, Sebastian."

"I should feel rewarded that you did before stealing from me and blackmailing me that you would out me as the artist to the world?"

"Whether it was a reward or not, I don't know. But I'd never done that before and that—"

"You did not do what before?"

"Sleep with a man after knowing him for a few hours. Or sleep with any man," she added, though she immediately wished she hadn't. All this intimacy between them, it was forced by circumstance, not mutual want. In the normal world where she dwelled, she would have never gotten this close to Sebastian Skalas, nor should she want to.

"So you might think it's some cunning plan to seduce you but it wasn't. The moment you noticed me and started speaking to me, I lost control of everything. Including myself."

For a long while, he didn't say anything. Frustration coiled around Laila's heart. The man had a knack for making her own up to all kinds of things and yet clammed up just when she needed him to say something. But she'd come this far, so she might as well say the rest. "I stand by what I did to protect Guido from you. But I wish I didn't have to do any of it. I would have come to you ages ago to tell you about the boys if not for the history between us. How can you insist on any kind of relationship between us when what I did will always color your thoughts, Sebastian?"

"Do you want me to forgive you, Laila? Or beg for forgiveness myself? Will it clear the slate between us?"

"I don't know," she said honestly.

He pushed a hand through his hair. "It is enough if I admit that I understand why you did it, *ne*?"

"But I want to—"

"How about we call a truce, Dr. Jaafri?" he said, interrupting her. "For the sake of our sons, we will start afresh, as much as possible. We will leave our misguided reasons behind and move forward."

It was the best she was going to get out of him—that almost admission of guilt. Something about the resolve glinting in his eyes made her ask, "What if Zayn takes longer to get close to you? To trust you? Will you abandon the whole venture then?"

Gray eyes held hers. "Patience *is* one of my virtues, Laila."

"What isn't?" she said, his words pinging over her skin.

"You'll find out soon enough," he said, his eyes taunting her yet again. "This is a novel experience for me, too. There are very few times in my life that I have set my mind to something."

"With Zayn…" Laila said, trying to parse through to the meaning in his words, "respecting his boundaries is very important and for a man who's had nothing to do with children, you made it seamless. My mother and sister usually…" She hesitated, loath to dump her frustration with them on his head.

He sat up slowly, like a predator uncoiling itself from its resting stance. "Usually what?"

"They…crowd Zayn. They constantly demand he talk to them or force playing on him or pick him up when he doesn't like to be touched. The whole thing riles him up and then he digs down into his bad mood. It usually takes me two to three days after they leave to reassure him that I won't encroach on him like they did, to get him back to a routine."

"Why not talk to them about respecting his boundaries?"

Laila scoffed. "Two-year-old with boundaries? My mother doesn't even acknowledge mine. You should have seen her reaction when I told her I was having the babies."

When the silence continued to build and he watched her steadily, Laila flushed. "Why does your silence feel like you're holding back?" she bit out.

He laughed then and this was different. This was real, with a jagged edge to the sound, as if it *had* caught him by surprise and he didn't have enough time to run it past a filter. The Charming Playboy filter. "You're very clever and perceptive, *ne*? Glad our boys have one parent to inherit smarts from."

"I know better than anyone who you are, Sebastian. But since reminding you of how I know that might spoil the mood, I shall not. Why did you laugh?"

"Because you pinned me spot-on. If you marry me, I can deal with your mother. I can deal with anyone who doesn't respect my son's boundaries. Zayn is just as special as Nikos," he said with such sudden aggression in his words that Laila felt like he'd sliced open her biggest fear for her sensitive son. "I'd hate for *anyone* to make him think otherwise."

His fierce support of Zayn made emotion surge through her. The yogurt felt sticky in her throat. "I agree. If I thought Mama or Nadia were causing him harm, I'd cut them out of our lives without another thought."

He nodded. But even their mutual agreement seemed to stir up tension between them.

Laila felt it in the pit of her belly, a taut thread tugging her this way and that. It was so new to her…this restlessness simmering under her skin. Along with the long, emotional day she'd had, it was a bit much to take in. Her breath shuddered as she tried to contain all the different emotions vying for attention.

Two seconds later, she almost jerked out of her chair when gentle fingers danced over her ankle. She looked up to find Sebastian had moved to a closer chair in front of her. "What are you doing?"

"You've had a long day," he said, bringing her foot to rest on his thigh. When she remained stiff in his hold, he looked up. "It's okay. You can let go for two minutes."

She hadn't cried on long, hard nights when it felt like the boys would never settle or when her career seemed to stall because she couldn't give it her hundred percent and when the bills seemed to pile on. And yet now… A sudden sob burst through her. Swallowing against it felt like fighting an incoming tide and a small part of her wanted to drown.

She could feel his shock in how his fingers stilled. "Are you okay, Dr. Jaafri?"

Laila tried a mockery of a smile. "I'm sorry. I don't know what's wrong with me…the whole thing is hitting me now, I think, and…"

"You don't have to apologize. I understand," he said in such a tender voice that Laila forced herself to look away. She was afraid that that tenderness, real or fabricated, might just be her undoing.

Sebastian didn't let her think, though. He nudged her foot farther into his grasp and his nimble fingers pressed into her heel and the painful arch and the sore digits, and he was kneading and pressing with such gentle, firm strokes that she felt like she was floating away on some fluffy cloud, as far as possible from hard, cold reality.

Leaning against the back of her soft chair, she threw her head back and closed her eyes. The man could weave magic with those fingers, and not just on her feet. Tension lingered but more crept in—this languorous sense of well-being she had never tasted. With her heel tucked snugly against his abdomen, which was a slab of rock, something else stirred beneath the overwhelming relief. She groaned when he switched to the other foot, hitting an especially sore spot.

"Will you throw in these foot massages daily if I agree to your condition?" She meant to sound jovial. But her body betrayed her, making her words sound like a husky invitation.

His fingers stilled on her ankle. With a lock of jet-black hair falling onto his forehead, his mouth wreathed in that wicked smile again, he looked exactly how she'd dreamed of him for three years. "Try me and see, Dr. Jaafri."

Wordless, breathless, she pulled her feet back. When she stood up, tiredness hit her like a full-body slam at her martial arts class. "Thank you for…everything."

"I did no more than the minimum expected of me today."

"You really believe that, no?" she said, picking up her spoon and the empty bowls.

Reaching her, he took them from her hands. The simple contact of his fingers lingering on hers felt so good that she had to pluck hers away. "The staff will pick those up."

"Good night, Sebastian," she said and turned away.

Behind her, he said, "Why did you decide to have the babies?"

"Why do you think?" she said, feeling instantly defensive.

"Don't worry. In all this, there's one thing that's very clear. You seek nothing from me that's not solely for the boys."

Somehow, that didn't sound as reassuring as it should have. It felt more like…scorn or mockery.

"You said your mother disapproved of your decision and I can see why, at least partly." Suddenly, he was standing too close. "How old are you?"

Laila jerked her gaze up from the inviting hollow of his throat. "Twenty-seven."

He cursed. "So, you were twenty-four when you—"

"I already had tenure at university, a clear path for my career," she said, cutting his taunt off.

"At that young age?"

"I graduated high school very early, finished my PhD when I was twenty. Academics are easy for me," she said, expecting his surprise. "Socializing, and saying one thing but meaning another, playing the polite but backstabbing games with colleagues in academia, all the strange dating rituals…not so much.

"Romance wasn't in the cards for me. Then you and I happened. When I found out I was pregnant, with twins at that… It was terrifying at first. But… I also had Guido and Paloma and the safe space to really think it through."

"It was that easy to make that decision?"

"When I was a little girl, I used to pray and wish and

hope for a fun, boisterous, happy family, with parents who adored one another and siblings who loved each other. I wanted to be…loved and wanted as I was." She tried to scoff at her naïveté, afraid that he would do it, but couldn't.

"With the pregnancy, I realized this was my chance to make my wish come true. Even if the boys only had me, I thought…this is it. The logistics and reality were much, much harder than even my rigorous calculations," she said with a self-deprecating laugh, "but the love I see in Nikos's and Zayn's eyes when they look at me or reach for me or when they kiss my cheek with grubby mouths… I know I'm living my dream. No fear, or worry or overdue bill can take that away from me."

Sebastian walked impossibly closer, and her pulse began to race. She could see the deep, disorienting gray of his eyes, could smell his cologne and sweat, could feel the warmth of his lean body graze her muscles in a lazy invitation.

She held his gaze, some wild instinct she'd known only once before egging her on even as her belly took a dizzying dive.

"I've always wanted a family like that. Now we can both get what we want, *ne*?" His words were low, soft, as if he was tempering some great emotion. "You have only convinced me that I'm right, Dr. Jaafri. And soon, you'll agree."

Then, in a move that made her heart beat out a wild rhythm, his hands landed on her shoulders, and he pulled her to him.

Laila sank into the hard warmth of his body, trembling like a leaf in a storm. His arms felt like salvation, like a cocoon, like her very own safe place to land. And somehow, that deep sense of security seemed to open the floodgates to all the worries she'd been shouldering alone even before the boys had been born.

Soundless sobs shook her, washing away any embarrassment she should feel for breaking down in front of him. Sebastian didn't seem even a bit surprised or thrown off at her crying. His arms tightened, his lips whispering soft, sweet words in Greek, wrapping them around her like a safety blanket. His words, his touch, his warmth… It was a glorious gift she hadn't known she needed.

Relief filled her in soft, overwhelming waves, followed by sudden, thick fingers of sleep and she barely had a memory of sinking into his arms and the vague impression of him carrying her to bed and tucking her in, as if she too were precious to him.

Laila slept like the dead that night, thinking it curious that it was thanks to the same man who had kept her awake for countless nights.

CHAPTER FIVE

SOMEHOW THEY SETTLED into an easy routine over the next few weeks, though it should have been impossible on paper.

Not somehow, Laila acknowledged. It was thanks to Sebastian.

There wasn't a single thing that the boys or she needed that wasn't already arranged or sorted for them, before Laila herself could think of it. He'd arranged for Annika and Alexandros to leave the villa for a whole two weeks, so that the four of them could bond as a unit, even as he admitted that Alexandros had been quite put out about moving his very pregnant wife into his penthouse in Athens, even temporarily. Laila had thought it was also because Sebastian wanted to avoid Ani, but she kept that to herself.

She would have liked to have Ani around, to avoid too much one-on-one time with Sebastian. After her near breakdown and his tenderness that first night, Laila felt as if there was no equation or model for her feelings to follow. Unless it was chaos theory, since they went up and down and around, tying her in helpless knots. Apparently, a little kindness from Sebastian could make her as fragile as Nikos's sandcastle.

He had also forbidden their grandmother Thea from visiting just yet, Alexandros had quipped, expressly for Laila's sake. Being the traditional matriarch, Thea would apparently bear down on Laila to make her great-grandsons legitimate heirs of the Skalas family ASAP.

Laila had enough to handle with her world turning upside down, thanks to Sebastian's determination to mold himself into the father of the century and the most reliable, easygoing, close-to-wonderful co-parent.

He'd gone overboard with an army of extra staff he had interviewed himself and hired to keep an eye on the boys around the villa, and an insane number of toys and swings and slides and scooters and bicycles and inflatable castles that had begun to arrive in quick succession at the villa over the first week.

On the sixth afternoon of their arrival, Laila ran out, her heart in her throat, as Nikos shouted loudly for her from the front lawn. She skidded to a stop on top of the steps to find Sebastian on his knees, surrounded by two puppies and their sons, though Zayn was a few steps behind his twin.

Mouth hanging open, Laila reached them. "Sebastian, what did you do?" she asked, inanely.

Zayn answered for his father, more excited than she'd seen him in a long while, amber eyes dancing with pleasure. "Puppies, Mama." He held up two of his little chubby fingers aloft as if to make sure she understood the significance of the number. "Two puppies, one for Nikos. One for me," he said, thumping his chest, then turning away to run toward the tiny little bundles.

There was no way for Sebastian to answer her, though he grinned at her from the ground. Hair flopping onto his forehead, gray eyes shining with attention, he was overwhelmingly gorgeous, far too real in a way Laila had never imagined he could be. For one bitter second, she wanted to say he was manipulating the boys but she instantly knew that was unfair.

She followed the caravan—Paloma and the two helpers gleefully joining in—as Sebastian showed both the boys how to pet the tiny puppies and told them in soft, easy words how important it was to treat them kindly and to give them lots of love.

Nikos and Zayn—eyes bright and wide—followed his hands and his words and his actions, as if he was a larger-than-life hero. And maybe to her sons, he was a hero.

Maybe, sooner or later, they would have needed this, too, in their life. Laila had enough experience to know that one parent's undivided, unconditional affection could never make up for negligence from the other.

It was a long while—after he directed them to pour water in the puppies' bowls, and put a leash on them and set them all free—before Sebastian walked toward her.

Hair wind-ruffled, dark denim showing off his lean physique, he looked like he had walked out of a photo shoot. Wishing she'd put on a different top and combed her wayward hair, Laila rubbed at the banana stain on her shirt.

If he noticed her frantically grooming herself like

a pet being presented to its master, thankfully he ignored it. She felt an instant thrum under her skin when he finally reached her, a thin sheen of sweat coating his face and neck.

"You didn't come to pet the puppies. The boys called you enough times."

Of all the things for him to notice and comment on… Laila was continually shocked by how perceptive he was for a shallow playboy who cared nothing about others. Or at least that was the impression he wanted to make. "I'm… I'm not used to dogs. In fact, I'm scared of them," she admitted, her cheeks going pink.

If she thought he'd laugh at her, he proved her wrong again. "You didn't have one growing up? Never played with a neighbor's dog?"

"No. I had enough people to look after without adding a dog to the mix," she said, before she could arrest the thin thread of resentment. "Baba was an academic who buried his head in research and history and my mother and sister… They would have hated the idea of a dog. Unless it was one of those posh crossbreeds that fits in a designer purse."

When he stared at her in surprise, she colored. "What about you? Did you have one?"

"No. I begged and begged but was not allowed. It was a sort of punishment."

"For what?"

"Let's just say I was a lot to handle as a kid. Giving me a dog would have been too much. And in hindsight, I'm glad I was deprived of it."

Laila stilled at the strange tenor to his words, the tight

set of his jaw. But she didn't want to probe. "You're a lot to handle even now," she said, hoping to pull him out of that dark mood.

Meeting her eyes, he grinned. For the space of a second, his gaze dipped to her mouth and then back up. "I'm easy to handle if one was inclined to learn," he said, his tone returning to teasing.

"Two tiny puppies, though, Sebastian?" she said, as much to cover the heat racing her cheeks as much to speak up. He flirted so easily with her and it wasn't like it was an act, either. She knew that much. "That's a bit much for two-year-olds, don't you think?"

"A boy should always have a dog."

She heard both his resolve and something more—like a loss—in those words. It shook her a bit, the intensity he hid beneath his easy charm. "Who's going to look after them? They're babies."

"All of us."

"You're spoiling them," she said, unable to help sounding critical.

"I have more than two years to make up for." He turned to her, turning that thousand-watt attention squarely on her. Her skin prickled. "What's really bothering you, Dr. Jaafri?"

Their gazes held in a silent battle before she relented with a sigh. "Puppies feel permanent. It will be hard enough to make the boys understand when…if things don't work out."

His anger was betrayed by the tight fit of his mouth but nothing more. "I don't think you've still grasped my commitment to this and maybe that's on me. To answer your question, if you move out of here, which will be because you didn't give this a fair chance, the puppies and the extra helpers and probably even I will just follow. That's how this works, *ne*?"

With a sigh, she nodded.

But whatever he thought of her doubts, he didn't let it linger. Shooting to his feet, he gave her his hand. Surprised, Laila took it anyway. His big hand enfolded hers in an easy grip as he tugged her. "It's time you learn to play with puppies, Dr. Jaafri. Come."

"What? No. I mean… That's not necessary, Sebastian. The boys have you and everyone else to help them."

"Not to help. But for fun. For yourself."

Shocked, Laila offered no more protest and soon, her sons were shouting that she had joined and two adorable puppies were licking her chin and Sebastian laughed and held her when she burrowed into him when the more aggressive one tried to climb her legs.

Hard and hot and smelling of clean sweat and a subtle cologne, he was more than a safe haven. Under the guise of hiding from the teeny puppy, Laila clung to him for a few more seconds, and when she looked up into his gray gaze, she knew that he knew.

But he didn't mock her. With a warm flame in his gray eyes, he tightened his arms and Laila wondered at how easily he made her feel wanted.

With each passing day, Laila felt more and more out of control of her own life, even though she was doing so much more than the bare minimum. Which was strange because she was less worried about the boys' long-term security now, and had three whole hours every afternoon to focus on the paper she was writing for an extremely competitive academic journal. Paloma had two new helpers, other than Sebastian being on hand, if the boys didn't settle down for their two naps, *and*, she knew 100 percent that she'd made the right decision.

The boys were thriving under Sebastian's patient presence. Though Zayn wouldn't come out and show it just yet.

Her sensitive son watched his papa and his twin play and run and chase dogs with his big, thick-lashed amber eyes wide and curious and longing, quite how Laila watched Sebastian, she imagined. Desperate to be part of them, but not yet ready to join in, or not knowing how.

While she was beginning to believe that Sebastian had the boys' best interests at heart, Laila thought that exact reason boded something else for her.

"I've always wanted a family, too," he'd said and meant it.

Which, quite logically, led her to believe that he would do anything to persuade her to make them into a traditional family unit through marriage.

In his mind, she might as well be no more than a tool he would use to get close to his sons, to ensure their well-being and happiness, as easily as he might employ a dog or a toy. She could be any woman in the world—her defining role to him was that she was his sons' mother.

Which should be reason enough for her to resist the lure he cast. If not for her actively pursuing him, he would never have come into her orbit, never danced with her or taken her to bed. Never made an offer of marriage, if not for their sons.

Sebastian Skalas was like the sun, just as Mama once had been. He sparkled and glittered and drew others into his orbit automatically, for fun, for entertainment, wherever his fancy stuck. And then he moved on, leaving people like her sons discarded like broken toys. Just like Mama had done to Baba.

Just like he would do to Laila, given she was the exact opposite of the woman a man like him noticed.

And yet, for some inexplicable, possibly foolish and definitely naive reason that went against every bit of rationale she tried to dredge up, Laila wanted him to want her. She wanted to be seduced. She wanted more of his soft confessions and wicked smiles, and she wanted those strong arms that had wrapped around her with such gentleness to move all over her with desire and urgency and none of that smooth control.

She wanted more than his pretend hugs and polite bridge-building and fake friendship. She wanted to peel beneath the various masks he put on. Until she knew what he'd wanted from Guido so badly that he'd have ruined the older man. Until she knew why he hid his art from the world. Until she knew him like no one else did.

It was impossible to put this into a rational construct except that she'd clearly been a lot lonelier than usual since her pregnancy, and she wanted sex and companionship, and she wanted both of these specifically from Sebastian.

Whether it was because he was the father of her sons or because he'd been her only lover, or because something about him inexplicably drew her to him, she had no idea.

With a frustrated groan, she pushed away from the massive desk in the airy sunroom that had been created as her workspace. Three solid hours of free time and she was spending it daydreaming ridiculous scenarios about a man who only wanted her in his life for their sons. Leaving her to wonder what it was about Sebastian Skalas that always made her act out of character.

CHAPTER SIX

In hindsight, Laila thought she should have expected that Sebastian would default to form in that spectacularly dramatic fashion of his—getting caught smooching some tall, anemically thin, cheekbones-for-life model/designer/party girl.

Three weeks *was* a long time for him to act the domesticated homebody, given he'd spent most of his life in the most profligate of ways.

That some tabloid toe rag had caught him smooching said Slavic model wouldn't have been on Laila's radar, if Annika in her desperation to stop Laila from seeing it had inadvertently made Laila curious enough to seek it out.

In a smart black jacket with the white shirt underneath open to his abdomen, he had been caught in profile, with the model's mouth attached to his, her body wrapped around him like a squid's tentacles from the boys' favorite cartoon show. This was on the first night he'd been away from the villa since their arrival.

He hadn't yet returned from his jaunt and Laila wondered if he had to like…build a buffer of partying and sleeping around and causing general mayhem to sustain being the responsible, caring parent the rest of the time. Like her own mother, who'd needed parties and theater and flirting endlessly with "exciting men" because she claimed her life with Baba was boring and dull and predictable. As if it was his primary responsibility in life to provide entertainment for her. Failing that, she'd expected him to support her extravagant lifestyle.

This wasn't the same, Laila tried to tell herself. He hadn't made any promises of fidelity to her. He'd offered a cookie-cutter marriage deal that she hadn't accepted. He was free of obligation to her. They had nothing in common except the boys. He wasn't a man she could trust a hundred percent. Her excuses for him went on and on but didn't stick, didn't make the slice of hurt lessen.

Seeing him with his…flavor of the month felt like someone had picked her up and thrown her across a hard floor. Like her very breath had been beaten out of her. Like the numerous times when her half sister, Nadia, had teased her that she didn't belong with her and their mother because she was so…weird with her "not-so-slender build and over-smart brains" and a freak with her head buried in numbers and models.

Laila's first instinct was to pack up the boys and run away, which was laughable in itself because where would she run to and from what. And she wasn't the sort to run away from reality in the first place. This was her life now, even if disappointment clung like bitter bile to the back of her throat. What she needed was to get out of the villa, at least for a short while. Meet someone from her plane of reality to get her head screwed on right.

After all, this villa and the lifestyle and the man himself… They could all be from an alien planet she'd been thrust into.

She made arrangements with Paloma and her helpers early next morning so that she could have the afternoon for herself. She refused Annika's offer to accompany her on her "shopping trip," having already divided Annika's loyalties enough to cause the rift of a lifetime. Sebastian was still avoiding her and the last thing she needed was to disclose her thorny feelings about him to her.

When Alexandros commanded in that steely voice of his that he'd arranged for a chopper to bring her to Athens, she'd almost lost her temper at him. But he wasn't her culprit. And she was working hard on convincing herself that no one was.

Finally, after what felt like an eternity but really was maybe thirty minutes, the chopper dropped her off on top of a skyscraper in the business district of Athens, close enough to the café that was her destination.

Laila took the elevator down to the boutique Annika had recommended. Not that she could afford anything more than a pair of shoelaces there, but to kill time before her friend was due.

When she stepped onto the sprawling thirty-second floor, with its shining mosaic floors and all-glass facades—clearly home to a host of exclusive, designer stores—the entire level was suspiciously empty. As was the boutique with its gleaming black marble floors, pristine white counters and a lingering expensive scent that made Laila feel like a wild creature in the plastic jungle.

Looking around the quiet space, she wondered if

she'd somehow missed a local holiday. On further inspection, she found the boutique to be open, with a tall, stylish woman hovering around the entrance, looking at Laila as if she was a royal dignitary gracing the boutique with her magnanimous presence.

"Dr. Jaafri? Welcome," the woman said. "I'm Natasha. The store and I are at your disposal for the next several hours."

Laila opened her mouth, closed it, then followed the woman into the store. Now, she felt churlish for refusing Ani's company when she'd clearly arranged everything for her. She spent the next hour pleasantly surprised when she tried out the collection of frothy silk dresses, soft-as-butter blouses and trousers she preferred for work that the woman picked out to suit her unusual frame of wide shoulders, small breasts and hippy…hips.

Even though she couldn't really keep any of the pieces, Laila gave in to the pleasurable folly of trying dresses that were utterly unsuitable for her lifestyle and way out of her price range. Neither did she miss the fact that at these astronomical designer price tags, even her body could look damn good.

Two glasses of the most delicious champagne and two macarons later, she felt giddy enough to try a daring sleeveless little number in a burnt orange shade that did wonders for her golden brown complexion. The bodice was pretty much a strap around her breasts and then flared, falling a couple of inches above her knees, showing off her long legs.

Having thanked Natasha for helping her into it, Laila was about to look at herself when her nape prickled. She turned and heard the woman leave the room immediately, the door closing behind her.

Sebastian stood inside the room, immediately shrinking it in size.

In a leather jacket and dark denim that hugged his long legs, he looked like he could be one of the perfectly proportioned mannequins. Except no man made of synthetic materials could hold that warm, wicked light his gray eyes did. He looked how she imagined he'd look after a couple of nights of debauchery. Dark shadows clung to his eyes and there was at least two days' worth of stubble on his jaw. Despite his disheveled state, there was a faint buzz of sensuality that emanated from him, as if he couldn't help putting that particular vibe out.

Had he rolled out of that model's bed an hour ago? Had he come here with that woman's scent on him?

The tacky, jealousy-filled questions gave her whiplash as she fought to tamp them. *None of my business* didn't really seem to work.

Even the fact that he might have been with another woman not an hour ago could diminish his appeal, though. She had to consciously work on tugging her gaze away from the V of his T-shirt, from the corded column of his throat, that hollow she desperately wanted to…lick and smush her face against.

"Did you miss me, Laila?"

"Excuse me?"

"You have that look in your eyes, the one that says you want to inhale me whole."

Heat crested her cheeks. "That's probably the champagne on an empty stomach. What are you doing here?" Suddenly, the empty building made sense.

"Alexandros informed me about your sudden expedition. The building was evacuated. I had this store open since Ani said you wanted to shop here."

She swallowed and looked around. So, Natasha and the little surprise had been his doing? Because he wanted to assuage a guilty conscience? "Isn't that a bit much?"

"Given there were hordes of reporters here half an hour ago, I would say not."

"Reporters?" she repeated blankly. "Here? Why?"

"I'm not fond of saying I told you so. Smacks of self-righteous pride. I believe it might be because news got out that I have sons." He pushed off the wall with a smooth grace, immediately giving her the impression that he was on the chase and she was his prey. "Alexandros said he barely got you to take the chopper. You should have—"

"I didn't realize I was under house arrest. Or that I need your permission every time I need a break."

Hands tucked into the back pockets of his trousers, chin tucked down, he stared at her. "Something is wrong. Is it Zayn? Has Nikos—?"

"They're fine. Though Nikos won't stop asking after you."

Just like that, the exhaustion clinging to him vanished, changing the panorama of his face. "And Zayn?"

Two simple words and the entire universe seemed to expand with the hope pulsing within them.

For a second, Laila considered lying, then abandoned

the idea. Sebastian's devotion to his sons was a rare quality and his actions toward her shouldn't be her barometer to judge him. It was easier said than done, though. "You know how his little body stills and he won't even blink when he's really invested in something?"

Sebastian nodded.

"He gets like that every time Nikos asks after you."

His chest rose and fell, his lips pursing inward and then out. And then in the blink of an eye, he switched personas. "I hear you have a hot date. Is that why you're shopping?"

"I'm meeting a friend for a drink." When he watched her, unblinking, as if she was hiding state secrets, she said, "I thought the advantage of this whole arrangement was that I could take a couple of hours out of my life for myself."

"Of course it is. Unless you told this friend who the boys' father is, and he leaked it to the press."

"Fahad would never do anything that would hurt me."

"Maybe not," Sebastian said, getting a belligerent look in his eyes that she was beginning to recognize as possessiveness. "Then how would we explain why the press was coming after you today? Alexandros doubled the security around the villa."

"Maybe they were here because they wanted to get a look at you and your arm candy?" Laila burst out.

"My arm candy?" With a curse, he rubbed his hand over his face. "You saw the tabloid?"

"It's none of my business."

When she tried to move forward, he blocked her, his

hand on her elbow. Even disheveled, the man packed a punch with his magnetic presence. “You aren’t upset, then?”

She shook her head, avoiding his gaze.

“If I tell you that she came onto me and kissed me, and the photographer caught us right as I untangled myself? That I have no interest in her or anyone else? That she and some friends orchestrated that whole scene in some stupid welcome joke since I’ve been MIA?”

Laila folded her arms, feeling that strange tension gather in her belly again. It was that irrational, inconvenient want she felt near him. “It doesn’t matter, Sebastian.”

He leaned in closer, trapping her against the glass wall behind her. “It doesn’t matter that I propose marriage to you and then turn around and sleep with the first woman I come across that’s not you?”

Laila stilled, sensing a sudden change in the very air around them. He was…angry. Blisteringly so. He hadn’t been this angry when she’d revealed the news about the boys. And she knew instantly that she had made a mistake, that she had rubbed salt on a wound that clearly festered. “Since I didn’t accept your proposal, it’s not…”

He laughed then and it was so bitter that she felt nauseated. His lean body tightened with tension. “Maybe Alexandros is right that I’m a fool to offer you all that I have.”

Laila didn’t give a damn what Alexandros thought. She did care, however, that she had misjudged Sebastian through her own insecurities and created strife between them. "I hate to say this but your history made me believe the clip, Sebastian. You're notorious for this kind of behavior, for changing partners on a whim, for chasing every high, for excessively wild risks. What was I supposed to do when you disappear after three weeks with us and then show up with a woman clinging to you plastered all over the internet?"

"You could have asked me. Or is my word not trustworthy, too?"

"If you say you didn't kiss that woman, you didn't kiss that woman," she said, rushing through the words. "But we're…opposites. You thrive on excitement, and risks and bending society's rules and I'm a boring, dull statistician whose deepest, darkest wish is to stay in and listen to old maestros on precious records. That's why your proposal won't work. You'll eventually tire of me."

"All of this based on a gossip rag that caught me at a bad moment?" His tone could cut through glass and she knew this was the real Sebastian.

"All of this based on a relationship that I've once seen go up in flames, where the…parties were just like us," she said, biting her parents' mention at the last second. "We have nothing in common except the boys."

"Oh, wow, so this is the statistician extrapolating data?"

Laila sighed. "You ended up at a raucous party the first night out in three weeks. You…were itching to get away the last few days. You…"

"Because I was beginning to get one of my bloody migraines. It's not a pretty sight for anyone and they claw me under for a few days. I didn't want to frighten the boys or you. And I ended up at the bloody party because I wanted to come back to the villa and needed something to numb the pain. Like an edible. It's the only thing that helps."

Suddenly, his disheveled state, the dark shadows under his eyes, the faint tension thrumming around him made…so much sense. Why hadn't he told her? "I'm sorry. I didn't know that you suffered from—"

He stepped back from her, shaking his head. And Laila had the suddenly dawning fear that she had lost something that she didn't know she needed—his willingness to build something between them. That fear made her articulate something she'd have never allowed herself—a right to him and his secrets, to his real self. "You could have told me you were unwell. Or that you needed to get away, that you get…restless when it begins. Just one line, Sebastian and all of this could have been avoided. How do you think a marriage would work between us if you won't even give me that at this stage?"

"I will not spend another half of my life trying to prove who I am or what I'm capable of."

The bitterness in his words, the flyaway tidbits she gathered about his childhood from Annika, his disinterest in anything related to the Skalas name, his refusal to share himself with the world as a renowned painter… She was operating blind on an emotional minefield. But the thing she knew with a sudden clarity was that she wanted a map to him. She wanted to reach him.

"You said we would start over and that can't be done if you hide parts of your real self from me, and show me the charming mask you put on for the rest of the world.

The boys need a father who will not hide away imperfect parts of himself. What do you think that says to them?"

A soft hiss escaped his lips and Laila knew she'd reached him. But there was more and she let it pour out. "I can't be in a relationship with a man who won't even give me easy communication in such small things. We might as well call it quits now."

His gray gaze pinned her to the spot, something dancing there. "Fine. This is my fault a hundred percent and I apologize. But instead of demanding an explanation, you decided to invite your boyfriend here in some twisted revenge?"

"Fahad is not my boyfriend," she said, suddenly understanding his anger.

"But he would like to be, no?" he retorted, with an unnerving perception.

Laila's shocked silence said things she didn't want to say.

He thrust a hand through his hair, a hardness she hated entering his eyes. "I will make other arrangements for you to stay close to the villa while I start custody proceedings. I know you won't believe it, but I'll be fair."

"I don't want that," she whispered, grabbing his arm, the resonant truth of her words dawning on her. "I invited him because he's from my world, Sebastian, and one of the few people who doesn't treat me like a freak. I needed to find the ground under my feet."

He stilled, as if her very touch was repellant. "You can't have it both ways, by holding some unnamed condition over my head then coming to the worst conclusions in your head. You agreed to give this a fair chance."

"You can't go off to parties with models without telling me why, either, Sebastian. Or better yet, just don't go to parties with models," she burst out, and then cringed at how demanding and possessive that sounded. The words lingered between them, dancing over a line she wished she had the strength to not cross. Laila pressed her forehead to his arm and exhaled. His hand in hers was big, rough, broad, and something about the touch anchored her. Gave her strength to be honest with him and herself, as strange as that sounded to her rational mind. "I…if I'm to give our bet a real consideration, if I am to believe that a marriage between us has a chance of working, you should know I…want fidelity, Sebastian. I want it to be as real as we can make it. I can't even consider doing it any other way."

"Noted, Dr. Jaafri," he said and the serious tone of his voice told her he understood the step she was taking.

"I convinced myself it did not matter if you kissed another woman," Laila went on. "I promised myself that I wouldn't let this become personal between us, wouldn't let my weakness for you…muddy this."

"Your weakness for me would blind you to who I am?"

She scoffed, her lips trembling at the dense muscle packed in his arm. "No. It blinds me with my own insecurities. It confirms patterns that I seek to protect myself with, even when they aren't there," she admitted with little grace.

"Look at me, Laila."

She raised her eyes, feeling as if she'd cracked herself open past a door that had always been inaccessible to her.

His eyes searched hers, a steely resolve to them. "Nikos and Zayn adore you. They will believe everything you do. You owe it to me to be careful how you judge me."

"That's the thing that sticks in my craw. When it shouldn't," she said, with a snort. "You see me as nothing but their mother. I could be any woman from the long list of your lovers and you would offer me the same little package deal." She pressed a hand to her chest, her heart thundering in there. "Apparently, I'm selfish enough in all this to not want to be a placeholder."

"You think I invited you into my home, my brother's home, into our private lives, without knowing what kind of a woman you are? Without considering the fact that you nearly ruined me and yourself out of loyalty for a man who's not even related to you? Without considering that you're not only devoted to my sons, but would stand up to me if I wasn't good enough for them? Without remembering that, amid all the lies you wove and the plans you made, you responded to me with a hunger and need I have relived a thousand times over in three years?"

Laila stared, feeling more than foolish. Fingers of heat trickled through her, banishing every doubt for now.

Sebastian scoffed. "Unlike you and Alexandros, I trust my instinct. As for not seeing you…" He rubbed a hand over his lower lip and she was beginning to see it for the tell it was when he wanted her. "You live under my roof and you follow my every move with those big eyes, just as hungrily as Zayn does. You seduced me and disappeared for three years, leaving me a damn note while I obsessively looked for you. I would plan what I'd do when I caught you so elaborately, dream of the moment I had in you in my hands… I'd see your face in every woman who was tall or had that way of walking or…" His warm breath coated Laila's lips. "It is already personal between us. It was, even before the boys."

Laila felt a liquid longing well up within her at his soft words. She felt greedy, grasping, voraciously so, for more from him. *Of him.* As much as it had been an act, the one night she'd spent in his company had been the most alive she'd ever felt. The most she had lived in her entire life.

It was a dangerous game to want to matter and she had lost before and yet… She felt like Paloma's yarn when the boys got their hands on it, unspooling away into sensations and feelings, tangling into knots, changed forever.

"What would you have done with me if you had caught me?"

CHAPTER SEVEN

HE SMILED AND it contained a multitude of promises and invitations. As if she'd asked him to reveal the secrets of the universe only to her and he'd been hoping she would ask. In that smile, Laila thought she could see her entire future, and the absurd thought nearly paralyzed her.

Grabbing her wrist, Sebastian said, "Come."

She let herself be dragged as if she was made of not bone and flesh, but want and longing. She giggled like she'd have as a normal teenager stealing away with a boy she liked, if that boy hadn't paid attention to her only because she was gateway to meeting her beautiful older sister, Nadia.

Taking her hand, Sebastian drew her inside a very upscale, very luxurious room painted in shades of soft pink and white. An intricate, vast chandelier hung from the high, round ceiling. Expensive and frothy-looking confections in bright silk—she supposed they were dresses—hung from a couple of rolling stands.

A rich purple velvet lounger stood in the middle of it, with trays of sweets and a bucket of champagne strewn about the room as if they had been expecting a…special guest.

"You planned this."

Sebastian didn't answer.

She busily mapped his broad back and his tapered waist and the outline of his buttocks in his black trousers with shameless greed, while he went around the large room turning on every light until Laila's reflection glowed in the three-fold full-length gold-edged mirror.

Since she'd left her hair to air-dry, her curls framed her face in what Mama called untamed, unsophisticated wildness. The deep rust-colored dress brought out the gold in her skin, clinging to her body just enough to hint at her small curves. Tiny golden hoops and a thin gold chain added just enough style. Her transformation from her usual food-stained loose T-shirts and shorts to this was by no means a Cinderella makeover.

But now, standing still under such soft, forgiving lights, forced to consider her reflection, Laila saw the changes in herself. Her pregnancy had left no big mark on her frame except her breasts were a little bigger. Her body had bounced back pretty easily, given she'd birthed twins, and she'd always been grateful for that.

Thanks to good genetics—which her mother bemoaned she hadn't inherited more of—she had glowing, golden-brown skin and the little lip gloss she'd borrowed from Annika made her wide mouth shimmer.

Whatever stress she'd carried along for months, weighing the biggest decision of her life, swinging back and forth, giving her a pinched look, was gone. Add the last month in with no worries about her finances or her career or the boys' well-being, the carefree nature of her present days showed in her face, as if she'd shed layers of skin. Though nowhere in the realms of Annika or her mother and sister, Laila thought she looked pretty just then, with her amber eyes glinting with excitement, her face made of strong, distinct angles, and confidence that came with living life the way she knew best, with making decisions that were right for her and her two sons.

Sebastian came to stand behind her, his head cocked to the side, his hands hovering over her shoulders but not landing.

Completing the picture, she thought, in a sudden bout of uncharacteristic whimsy.

"I told them to pamper you. There's a spa next door I was going to drag you to next."

"So that I can be brought up to scratch for you? For the Skalas family?" she asked, needing to know how much he cared about such things.

He met her eyes in the mirror, his gleaming with simple truth as he believed it. "Because beneath this brave, stubborn, calculating exterior lies a very beautiful woman who deserves the best."

"No need for false flattery," she whispered, even as she loved the thrum of anticipation through her body. "You've already caught me."

"Have I?"

"I… I've tried to relive that night, too. I've never been hornier, and I don't have enough sexual experience to know how to keep that separate from what we're trying to build with the boys. I know it's possible but I'm just not…sophisticated enough." She rushed on, her pulse dancing all over her body like an unearthed spark of electricity. "I left the villa today because seeing you lip-locked with that woman took me out at the knees. I needed to get you out of my head."

"What if we can keep them separate? What if I promise you that whatever happens between us, the boys are outside of this? What if you let us explore this between us? Admit it, Dr. Jaafri. A part of you loves risks just as much as I do. Or you wouldn't have played such an elaborate ruse on me."

She met his eyes, and the fight went out of her, leaving her boneless and free like never before. "You don't want any other woman?"

He shook his head.

"You want me?" she asked next, needing confirmation.

"Yes."

"Show me," she demanded, feeling a boldness she'd never felt before.

He pressed closer.

Laila closed her eyes, better to absorb all the delicious sensations assaulting her. Sweat and spice, he smelled like the decadent brew she used to relish when she'd been at college. Chest to thighs, he was hard and hot against her, his breath making the hair rise on the nape of her neck. Slowly, his arms came around her waist, as if he meant to gather her whole.

Laila stiffened.

"Shh… I can hear the gears in your head churning," he said, crooning at her ear, pulling her closer, his broad hand dancing across her not-so-flat belly. "You're gorgeous, Laila." One blunt-nailed finger traced the distinctive shape of her cheekbones, her too-large nose and her wide mouth as if he were memorizing the lines and details. "But more than that, you're fascinating and complex and brave." He rubbed his cheek against hers and the bristle scraped her skin deliciously. "You don't know what a draw that is for me. So, stop trying to put this into some equation and just…feel."

Exhaling on a shuddering breath, Laila relaxed. How an embrace could feel so arousing, she might never find out, but it was like an electrical charge running through her. Slowly, her back melted into his chest and a soft hiss escaped her mouth. His erection was a hot brand, notching up against her behind. One corded arm sidled up to lie under her breasts and then she was fully engulfed by him. His breath, his hands, his lips wound her up.

Feeling dizzy and drunk, Laila looked at his reflection in the mirror.

Those sharp cheeks dusted with dark pink, his nostrils flaring, his shapely lips slightly open, Sebastian looked as drunk on desire as she felt. The gray of his gaze deepened, into a maelstrom of hunger and need. He thrust his hips just a little and the little thrust sent damp warmth straight to her core.

"I walk around with my cock at half-mast when you strut around in those shorts, when your T-shirt gets wet during bath time, when you compulsively lick the honey from your lips every single night. When you sound sleepy and husky in the middle of the night when you check on the boys, and your hair is a halo around your face. When you're so exhausted that you can't help but lean against me and I can feel your warm, soft, silky skin." His fingers drew tantalizing trails all over her flesh—up and down, from left to right—as if waking up every nerve ending. As if it was all he'd wanted to do for a long while. "You disappeared on me and I couldn't get you out of my head. I haven't felt the faintest interest in another woman in three years. You have become an obsession." He nudged his hips against hers the same time as his hands pulled down the side zipper of her dress.

Laila groaned as his rough, broad hand completely engulfed her breasts. Her nipples poked at his palm, boldly demanding attention. "Is that enough proof for you, Dr. Jaafri?"

"Yes." Laila wanted to burrow into him. "I want more, too, Sebastian."

His long fingers kneaded and cupped her breast without touching her as she needed. "I will not be your stud because you're horny after three years of celibacy."

"I don't know how to prove to you that I'm horny *for you*," she said, half sobbing, half delirious with pinpricks of pleasure.

He laughed and it was suddenly imperative that she taste that smile.

Turning her head, sinking her fingers into his hair, she caught his lips with hers. She didn't have words like him, but she had this…deep, insistent longing to steal something of him for herself, to captivate him as he had done to her three years ago, to leave a small, indelible mark on him as he'd done to her. She traced the seam of his lips with soft, susurrating kisses and when he groaned roughly, she snuck her tongue into his mouth.

He tasted of whiskey and mint and of decadence and

pleasure she had rarely allowed herself. Pleasure she had only tasted because of him, wanted because of him.

She sucked the tip of his tongue, bit his lower lip, then licked the hurt. She devoured his mouth as if he was a feast she'd been waiting for, for so long. She pulled and tugged at his hair, raked her nails over the nape of his neck until his mouth was hers to do with as she wished.

He cursed when she let go for breath and then he was devouring her, hard and fast and deep, his erection pressing insistently against her behind.

She'd relived that moment from three years ago in her head for so long and now, she wanted him deep inside her and this time, she would own her pleasure instead of feeling guilt and shame around it. She would demand everything he was and wield everything she was at him without lies and half-truths.

"Is that enough proof for you?" she said, in a breathy voice that told its own tales and gave its own proof.

Clasping her cheek in one broad hand, Sebastian grinned against her mouth. Their rough exhales joined and created a symphony of their own. "Yes."

"Now, can we please proceed to this pampering thing you planned for me?"

"Yes," he said, loosening his hold on her.

Laila grabbed his corded arms. "I want it at your hands."

"At my hands? I might ruin you for anyone else, Dr. Jaafri."

"I dare you to try," she said, grinning, and saw his gaze flare with challenge.

* * *

Sebastian hadn't meant to seduce her today, here. Not that his mind was ever *not* planning how to get Laila under him, or over him, or against the wall.

Over the last three weeks, it had become as natural as wanting to see Nikos's wide grin, feeling Zayn's soft gaze land on him like an ever-present buzz. Like breathing and eating and walking and waking and sleeping and thinking of his art.

Wanting Laila had already been an obsession, now it was torment, too.

The more he wanted her, though, the more Sebastian restrained himself, as if warned by some strange instinct whispering in the back of his head. Usually, such control was…not in his nature.

He'd lived most of his life becoming a profligate wastrel, giving in to all kinds of excesses, doing his best to shame the Skalas name, and when the noise in his head got so loud that he couldn't bury it anymore in his wasted living, he painted.

He'd never set out to be a painter, as much as Konstantin had liked to taunt him that he'd done it for express purpose of pissing on him and the prestigious family name.

In truth, Sebastian had spent a lot of his adolescence fighting the art that seemed to want to get out of him, like some poison that needed to be purged, or skin that needed to be shed. In the last few years, he'd even let his brother and Thea and friends lead him into things he had no vested interest in, for lack of anything more important that engaged his interest.

But all that had changed with his sons' arrival. With Laila's spectacular reentry into his life. He had a desire now—as bright and hot like a flame—and he had a plan to fulfill that desire.

Detours and deep dives and self-destructive plays were not allowed. He wished he didn't have to run away and hide when his migraines hit. That he didn't need to calm the buildup of that relentless clamor in his head by painting. But those detours were necessary since he didn't want to expose the pain he had to bear to Laila's or his sons' eyes.

Whatever she might say now, he couldn't let her see him like that, at his worst. Couldn't let her see the gaping void his mother's abandonment had left in him, couldn't let her see that Konstantin had managed to beat out his capacity to care, to be vulnerable, to bare himself to another in all his true tormented glory. Couldn't let her see that between them, his parents had destroyed his ability to connect like a normal man.

He'd spent so long letting it decay and rot with shallow pursuits and mockery of relationships that he knew he would not make the kind of husband Laila wanted. He doubted he could give her even the conditional happiness she was expecting from their convenient arrangement.

But he'd not let the dark void of his past destroy his future, he would not lose his sons. And that meant making sure Laila could trust him, giving her everything she needed to show her that she mattered in the logical way she understood.

His desire for her was not a lie and he would use that as his negotiating tool. He'd lusted after her for three years, been celibate the entire time—deep in his obsession with finding her—when sex had been an easy escapade all his life. For all that he had called her one, Sebastian had whored himself away from the age of seventeen, in return for escape from his own head. And yet, he had abstained for three years. He hadn't even wanted to look at another woman, much less seek out entertainment or escape.

It was as if his brain had had enough meat and material to occupy itself in search of Laila. As if on some instinctual level he had known that they were not finished.

The whole idea of scheming in the vague way he was doing and plotting each step carefully and then trying to stick to that plan… It was all very boring and self-depriving when he wanted to act on his gut. When he wanted to take advantage of the long glances and trembling gasps Laila didn't even know she was putting out.

The woman was as naive about her sexual appeal as she was no-nonsense about their arrangement. A part of him just wanted to take what she would so readily offer.

Ironic that Laila was trying to play by her instincts more while he was trying his damnedest to stick to a plan. And with the same gut instinct, he also knew that he would never need an escape from her. They would settle into the kind of matrimonial bliss that was a shallow mirror of what his twin had but that was one thing they both agreed on, didn't they?

He just had to have patience and deny himself a little more and appeal to her newly awakened instincts. To prove to her she needed him, wanted him, as much as he needed her and his sons in his life.

His momentary escape into his own thoughts cost him for Laila stiffened in his arms. When he met her gaze in the mirror, he was relieved to find it was not affront. But…concern that felt like a thorny prickle against his skin. He did not need or deserve her concern. He had spent his entire life without it.

She tightened her clasp on his wrist. "You went away somewhere. Is that a lingering echo of the migraine?"

He shook his head. "I was trying to figure out where to begin your ruin."

She laughed, having clearly decided to believe his lie. There was such a gentle generosity to her spirit that it shone out of every pore, like her skin was giving off an iridescent glow. Her large amber eyes glowed with naked desire and were so artlessly honest that it hurt to meet them in the mirror.

He stared at her, feeling a strange, overwhelming desire to steal that laugh for himself. It wasn't simple lust, for he knew how he'd twisted that beyond shape.

Sex for him had always been a momentary escape, a game to see how far he could go in his debauchery, a perversion to run away from the noise in his head, a constant chase to see if it would be enough to fight the need to emote on a canvas—which was what his painting had always been about. More an experiment than any kind of need to connect with another.

This was more. Different. A near-compulsive need to dig beneath that silky skin and learn all her secrets, to expose every nook and cranny of how she was made to his greedy eyes. The exact opposite of escape, for it filled him with renewed fervor and something that would sustain him for a long time. And when this need faded, they would have companionship, they would have their family.

"The end is a given, no? However it begins?" she said, with an eagerness that he wanted to devour. Her nipples peaked against his palms, making his mouth water.

He tucked her closer against him and had the pleasure of seeing her eyes glaze. "Yes, though I have decided to try on self-control for size."

"What does that mean?"

"That means we will pursue your pleasure, not mine." He rubbed one plump nipple between his fingers, and she arched into his touch. "And this counts as one wish I'm granting you, *ne*?"

"You're diabolical to ask me that now," she said, her words so husky that they pinged over his skin.

He tugged at the bodice until her breast in his hand was exposed to their sight and tweaked the dark pink nipple. Twisting himself around her torso, he rubbed his bristly cheek against the plump knot. "Say yes, Laila."

"Fine, but—"

Sebastian didn't let her finish.

This time, he kissed her. As he'd been wanting to do for three long years. He tasted her surprise and her soft gasp and then she softened under his mouth. In his arms. As if here, she was giving up all her rationale and all her fight, and simply caving to pleasure. Tart and sweet, her mouth invited him in with a passion he'd never known with anyone else.

With all the women he'd taken to bed, perversely, it was the Skalas name and the status, or the genetics that made him look the way he did that attracted them. He'd never allowed any woman closer than that. But Laila had jumped his defenses with her lies and her truths and had gotten far too close before he'd realized it.

With her, being wanted was a trip unlike anything he'd ever known, because she knew him and still wanted him. *Cristos*, it was a dangerous high he could chase for the rest of his life.

Sinking one hand into her thick curls, he tugged until she turned to face her reflection in the mirror. He ran his mouth over her jaw to the pulse at her neck that had been boldly taunting him for so long now. He licked at that pulse before pinching the sensitive skin between his teeth and she moaned loud enough for the woman waiting outside the door to hear.

She was unaware of how loud and wanton she sounded, lost against him, and Sebastian lapped this up, too. Feeling a potent mix of possessiveness and protectiveness, he clamped his palm against her mouth and said, "You want to see what I'd have done with you, right?"

She met his gaze, bold and brave. Always, so brave.

"This is between you and me, *matia mou*. And nothing to do with our arrangement or the future. Just the present, *ne*?"

She nodded, her curls bouncing this way and that, her front two crooked teeth digging into her lower lip.

"Tell me, Laila. Tell me what you would have me do with you. Choose your ruin, *yineka mou*," he whispered, feeling an abyss-like need for her surrender.

A fiery streak of red coated her cheekbones, like the tail of a comet painting the sky.

Would she leave devastation in her wake somehow?

The intrusive thought shook him up, before she caught his attention again. No, she wasn't going anywhere.

Her amber eyes glinted with flecks of gold, the irises blown up. "You're supposed to show me what you'd have done if you had caught me."

He grinned and licked the shell of her ear.

She writhed against him, her nails digging into his thighs, a perfect canvas for him to play on. "I'd have demanded your surrender," he whispered, caught up in the game. If the means itself could be so delicious and tormenting and full of pleasure, he would not even care about the end soon. "I'd have made you beg, *pethi mou*."

"Oh," she said, licking her lower lip with the tip of her tongue. "You seem to think I have ego invested in this, Sebastian. Wanting you and giving in—despite all the warnings and reasons I brought up to myself—was the easiest thing I'd ever done. The most pleasurable. When I learned that that night hadn't hurt anyone, that it wasn't cheating, I went home and cried."

"Why?"

"Because, for so many months, I shamed myself for thinking of you, over and over. I tried so hard to forget your touch. To stop thinking about you. But I couldn't. Nothing in my life has felt so good or so real as that night with you." She rubbed at her chest as if it burned now again and *Cristos*, he knew all about shame and she hadn't even done anything to feel it.

Sebastian covered her hand with his, loving how easily she gave up her feelings and her needs. He could get addicted to it.

She laced their fingers immediately, showing him trust he didn't deserve. "That first time after I saw how happy Annika was when she talked about Alexandros and then she said you were like a brother to her, it was as if all that shame and guilt had fallen off, leaving me free to…breathe and feel and want again. I went to bed and dreamed of you. I woke up during the night feeling achy and desperate for your touch. I…tried with my own fingers but it wasn't the same. So, I switched my phone on and googled you and there you were, splashed over the internet with woman after woman…and I…"

"It was all a show. You made escape impossible."

She shivered again, and he clasped her closer. "Make me feel like that again, Sebastian."

With a groan of his own, Sebastian thrust his hips into hers, rubbing himself against her curvy bottom. Holding her gaze, he filled one palm with her breast and sent the other down to explore.

She watched, as avidly as he did, when he rolled the hem of her dress up, revealing smooth, silky, thick thighs. *Cristos*, suddenly all he could think of was how she'd straddled his hips with those thighs. How he'd buried his teeth into the inner thigh. How she'd bucked and bowed when he'd laid his mouth on her core.

Panties made of some wispy silk covered her mound. Sebastian shoved the flimsy fabric aside and found her folds and her dampness. She was so ready for him, and it made him eager like he hadn't been even as a randy teenager.

"All this for me?" he said, gently probing at her entrance and dripping her wetness all over her folds.

Her thickly lashed eyes widened, and she must have smiled because they danced with a wicked pleasure and Sebastian suddenly loathed the fact that they were in public, when all he wanted to do was to strip her completely and drink in every nuance in her expression, every flicker in her eyes, every sweet word that fell from her lips.

"Keep your eyes on me," he said, and she instantly complied, like a kitten that knew it would get its reward.

Those big eyes held his, a promise and a demand and something more in them. He ran his mouth along her neck and her jaw, leaving a trail of wet kisses. And then he played with her damp folds. With his fingers inside her. With cajoling demands and whispered promises. With his mouth at her neck.

One arm wrapped around his neck, Laila undulated like a beautiful wave against him, rubbing that glorious ass against his shaft in a torment he wanted more of. Sebastian pinched her clit between his fingers, and she broke apart around him, digging those distinctly crooked front teeth into his forearm, her little gasps of pleasure so erotic that it left him shaking for relief and release.

Uncovering her mouth, he took it in a wild kiss. He lapped up the beads of sweat that had gathered on her upper lip, and he made her watch as he licked her taste from his fingers, and he made that blush appear again when he told her next time he was going to taste her directly. When her knees shook under her, he caught her, and when she hid her face in his chest and threw her arms around his waist with an artless, almost naive modesty, he felt a strange contraction in his chest that he buried along with a thread of unease that maybe, just maybe, for all her rules and caveats and logic, Laila did not know what she truly wanted, that something so convenient and conditional should not feel so good.

But he shrugged it away because what she truly wanted was in his power to give. For now, at least.

CHAPTER EIGHT

"WHAT IS IT that you want from my grandson, Dr. Jaafri?" Thea Skalas demanded, startling Laila out of a pleasant daydream where she broke Sebastian's new self-control like a sorceress and brought him to his knees.

She sat up and wiped her mouth with her napkin in case she'd been drooling, swallowing the foolish answer that rose to her lips for that first question. Given she'd barely had any sleep over the past few days—both boys had molars coming in—she hadn't seen much of Sebastian except in late-night silent meetups. Definitely not for any "only them" kind of encounters. Zayn clung to her during nights and while he was usually okay to play by himself during the day, it was Nikos's turn to want his Mama.

She was tired, cranky, horny and…confused. Sebastian had said he wanted to explore this thing between them, and yet, in a week, he hadn't made a move. He certainly seemed preoccupied with something. Laila wanted to ask him about him, but she was wary of making him think she was doubting him again.

The constant drama of her parents' marriage and her mother's erratic behavior every few weeks—her restlessness that either resulted in a reckless shopping spree or a night out on the city ending up at some wild party or calling up some old friend for a glamorous date—all those memories and the fears they'd left behind in her kept intruding on the decision she had made to trust him. The niggling feeling that she was right in her Baba's place, setting herself up for heartbreak, wouldn't leave her alone.

Which shouldn't be a problem at all because she wasn't involving her heart, right? At least, that's what she had told Sebastian. So why was she constantly looking at the past instead of moving forward with her own life?

There wasn't an hour that passed since that day at the boutique without her reliving the pleasure he'd strummed through her so easily. He'd even admitted that he hadn't wanted another woman in three years. Uncharacteristic enough for his lifestyle and the public playboy.

He gave of himself freely. Or at least he was smart enough to spin that illusion. Only now did Laila realize that he hadn't told her anything more about his migraines or what caused them or how long he'd had them. Neither had he let her bring Guido up again. God, she was going to drive herself half-mad with these circular thoughts.

And at the end of it all came anger with herself. Did she have so little trust in herself? As the old woman had pinpointed, what was it that Laila truly wanted?

"Dr. Jaafri?"

Laila sighed.

The reprieve Sebastian had been able to give her—from his grandmother, from the media, from the outside world—was apparently over and she only realized now how much effort he'd spent holding his twin and his grandmother, his family lawyers and the entire world at bay, so that she wasn't overwhelmed.

At breakfast this morning, Alexandros had mentioned the need to release a formal statement to the public regarding their presence in Sebastian's life, before the paparazzi got hold of the news and spun it into a narrative that none of them could control.

He talked of appointing a secretary for Laila who could organize her life to include things like photo shoots—because he insisted it was important to release a PR-approved photo of the boys and her and Sebastian to the media to reflect a "happy situation"—and schedule her travel. Because Laila *shouldn't* go back to the university or her Baba's old house or anywhere for that matter on her own willy-nilly. And to organize a party soon with all of the Skalas extended family and friends to announce Nikos and Zayn's joining the family.

All she'd been able to do was to turn to Sebastian like a helpless little fish flip-flopping on the land. The very idea of having a PA or performing little stunts for the media or having someone organize her very boring, very mundane life…was her worst nightmare come true. All of it bringing to head the constant doubts she chewed through about Sebastian and her belonging to different worlds, the constant taunts from Nadia that she didn't belong in her world and their mother's.

God, she hadn't even told her mother and half sister

for fear of having to face their reactions. For fear of cold reality crashing through whatever foundation she was trying to build with Sebastian.

Sebastian had responded by scolding his twin for ruining their appetites and informed him that Laila and he would come up with a plan together that was convenient and comfortable for them.

Before Laila could wrap her mind around all the things Alexandros demanded and how out of control her life suddenly felt, Thea Skalas had arrived, a month to the day since Laila had shown up.

The older woman's frail outward appearance had made Laila concerned for her until two minutes later, Thea had launched her campaign about the boys needing to be legitimized first thing at breakfast. The one thing Laila couldn't find fault with her was that whatever her beliefs about Laila, she'd openly and with tears flowing down her face welcomed Nikos and Zayn into the family.

"What would seal the deal in legitimizing my great-grandsons as Skalas heirs, once and for all?" Thea demanded, her impatience growing at Laila's silence.

Fortunately, Nikos and Zayn were seated far enough at the table now—near their papa and uncle that afternoon—so they didn't hear their great-grandmother's imperious demands.

"Grandmama!" Sebastian said, in a deceptively soft voice so that it didn't catch the boy's attention but delivered the warning anyway.

Thea turned her steely gray gaze toward him, even as she, too, kept an easy smile on her lips. "You might have spent your entire life mocking the Skalas name, Sebastian, but I know you damn well want it for the boys. Family matters to you too much to let it go. For whatever reason, you are letting her set the pace."

Family mattered to Sebastian.

It was an admission he'd made himself to her and yet, it landed in a different way falling from Thea Skalas's lips. Almost like an entity that held value in some abject form instead of gritty reality. Which she had handed him, part and parcel, by not only seducing him, then getting pregnant—yes, he'd played his part—*and* giving him two sons. Like he had himself ordered a nice, ready-made family off Amazon.

Sebastian turned to Laila, that small tilt to the right corner of his mouth.

Despite the unending string of questions in her head, that look he cast her was an instant injection of adrenaline. She adored it when Sebastian left the field to her—whether it was about the boys or other matters that concerned their life together—or when he didn't minimize her fears. For the first time in her life, she felt like she was part of something bigger than herself, like she belonged to a team or a unit, rather than operating alone as she'd done for so long.

"Maybe because he agrees with me," she said, addressing Thea, "that jumping into an outdated arrangement for the simple purpose of legality is less important than making sure the boys aren't caught up in something we're not ready for."

Thea pursed her lips while Alexandros said, "I

thought you were simply taking time to get to know each other."

Laila heard his poorly concealed outrage in his tone—he disliked the fact that his nephews were not legal Skalas family members yet. Thank God, Annika had been too tired to join them for this elaborate meal. She had no doubt her friend would take Laila's side in this particular argument, and it would only alienate Alexandros toward her even more.

The last thing Annika needed was more strife in her life because of Laila's…reluctance for matrimony. Neither was she unaware that her active resistance to the idea had already morphed into vague reluctance.

Sebastian peeled an orange and handed the juicy kernel to Nikos, who fed it to Zayn, immediately making a game of it, then stretching his pudgy palm toward his papa, for more.

"This matter is no one's business but mine and Laila's." Then he turned that intractable gaze toward his family members. "When did I ever give the impression that I will do as you two or the media or the entire damned world pleases?"

"I see you have him wrapped around your finger already. I must commend you for that," Thea said, shocking Laila yet again.

Something about her gaze said she meant it. She knew it was pointless to engage the older woman, but Laila couldn't help it. Plus, she wanted these people on her sons' side, which meant she needed them to respect her, if not like her.

"I have no intention of controlling Sebastian in any way. It's a partnership that I want."

"Ah… So you're a modern woman who doesn't respect the institution of marriage?"

"No, Grandmama," Laila said, testing the words on her lips. The older woman's gray eyes—so much like her grandsons'—gleamed with pleasure before she buried it.

"I have seen instances where it works—like Ani and Alexandros. And I have seen where it has burned down families. Sebastian and I have enough hang-ups without adding unnecessary, arbitrary structure to the mix. If I were you, I would back off. Because believe me when I say we're doing our best to make sure the boys have you all in their life."

Thea cackled and banged her palm on the table. "Fine, Dr. Jaafri," she said, respect glinting in her gaze. "You have my vote. If anyone can straighten out my useless grandson, it is you. Fate works in strange ways, *ne*?" she added as an afterthought.

Sebastian laughed, which set off Nikos chortling, which made him spew most of the orange he'd half chewed onto his uncle's shirt in a capture-worthy projectile.

Alexandros froze. Then slowly, he rubbed the toddler's face, then wiped some of Nikos's chewed-up orange from his shirt with a napkin. But the set of his face was so serious, his mouth so flat, that Nikos sobered up, watched around with those big eyes and, in two seconds flat, started wailing using all the lung power he had.

Laila sighed, knowing he was overstimulated. Her happy, easygoing baby never cried like that.

As Zayn watched his twin go off into a tantrum, his lower lip trembled dangerously but somehow, he held the incoming storm at bay, her brave, sensitive boy. Turning away from his uncle, Zayn handed another piece of orange to Nikos, who took it amid his cries and promptly started chewing on it, his chin now dripping with drool, snot and orange juice.

"*Cristos*, Alexandros!" Sebastian said, shooting to his feet with a violence she rarely saw in him. "It's just a piece of orange. You need not look like he did that to you on purpose, as if to insult you. He's just a little boy."

Alexandros Skalas, the mighty banker that all of Europe feared, looked like his brother had stricken him out of nowhere. "Of course I know that," he said, his tone whispery soft, even as he radiated tension. "I don't care if he…vomits on me, Sebastian. I'm not used to kids and I didn't even look at him straight because I was unsure of what to say or do and—"

"Yes, well. You better start learning how to handle them soon without that horrified, frozen expression or I'm going to have to raise your daughter, too," Sebastian threw back at him, only half-jokingly.

While Laila didn't much like Alexandros—so much for thinking they were similar—she felt a rush of sympathy for him. His expression made it clear that Sebastian's taunt hit where it hurt the most, and worse, it had basis in truth. Those gray eyes, so much like his twin's, watched Sebastian with such open envy that Laila had to look away. Thank God Annika hadn't been there to see it.

Laila turned to Sebastian, surprised at his cruelty

toward his brother. But her chastisement never formed on her lips.

With such tender care and patience that it caught even his grandmother's attention, Sebastian was busy wiping Nikos's mouth and hands with a wet napkin, all the while talking gibberish to him, trying to make him smile, and then picked him up out of his chair. He bent down to pick up Zayn, too, as if he'd done it for years, but pulled back at the last minute, face set into a fake smile he usually put on to show that Zayn's resistance didn't get to him.

The moment struck her again with the question that came to her in those rare, quiet moments where her thoughts wandered here and there. How endless was his capacity to feel that Zayn's reluctance to warm up to him still bothered him? Would he love a woman like that, too, or was it only limited to two innocent children, who were his blood and flesh?

Tucking Nikos against his side, he looked at Laila. "Nap and pool later? I'll get this one settled down," he said, switching Nikos from side to side as if he were a basketball.

Her firstborn giggled uncontrollably, causing a string of drool to drip over onto his papa's designer shirt.

Laila nodded, still in awe of Sebastian's near-miraculous capacity to love and care for his two sons.

He gave a nod to Zayn, always making sure to include him, then raised Nikos high above his head and swooshed him this way and that as he left the terrace. Her heart jumped into her throat and a protest rose to her lips, but Laila cut it off as she slowly picked up Zayn.

Her sons needed the safety of their papa's strong arms as much as they needed to learn to fly high and take risks, knowing in their hearts that he would never let either of them fall.

It came to her then—how this whole instinct thing worked. Because her trust in Sebastian's ability to be what Nikos and Zayn needed was absolute. If only she could feel the same sense of trust that he wanted her in his life…and as more than a part that would complete the vague picture he had for a perfect family. That day at that boutique, his admission that he hadn't wanted another woman in three years, that she'd become an obsession rang true, too. But obsessions were not…whatever it was that she wanted to be to him. It sounded too much like one of Mama's fancies, unreliable and bound to be replaced soon by a new one.

Neither could she forget that his "obsession" with her might have risen from the fact that she had pulled one on him. Once he had her assent to this marriage, once she unraveled for him in all the ways she couldn't resist, would he toss her aside? Would he push her to the margins of his life like he seemed to do with most everything and everyone? And if he did, was she okay with that?

For the first time in her life, Laila felt like her logic and rationale were of no use, and her heart definitely wouldn't follow her head.

The long summer day was finally coming to a spectacular end with the setting sun streaking the horizon with splashes of fiery orange when Laila decided to seek out Sebastian a few evenings later.

He had disappeared again, for a few days after Thea's arrival, although this time, he'd informed her that he'd be working and unavailable unless it was an emergency.

Laila had missed him—with even Zayn asking after his papa—and worried about him. Which, in itself was alarming because she was used to being alone, used to not needing to check in with anyone for days at a time. Even when Baba had been alive, he'd either be working or immersing himself in his books, putting together painstaking research on his favorite subject of Arab art of the nineteenth century.

Her intense dislike for playing the big boys' games at work meant she made few friends there. Outside of work, her life had been consumed by her sons. And yet already, she was too used to ending the day chatting with Sebastian. Already, she felt very little resistance about saying whatever came to her lips.

She had missed not only his steady presence with them, but also the wicked invitation in his eyes when he looked at her. When he rubbed the pad of his thumb against her lower lip. When she knew he wanted her but, for some reason, was playing a waiting game.

If he was struggling with another migraine coming on, she wished he would confide in her. But for all his seemingly open nature, there was a wall she sensed in him and a host of subjects that were forbidden to her.

When Paloma had informed her that he'd returned to the villa after the boys had been settled into bed this evening, she threw on a white cotton dress with halter neck straps, another perfectly fitting dress that had been delivered as part of her new wardrobe, and pulled her unruly hair back with a clip, chiding herself all the while for dressing for him.

But she refused to be brought down by the negative voice in her head—that she was only beginning to realize now sounded too much like Mama, as if she'd internalized all the things she was always saying to Laila in the form of "self-improvement advice."

Laila had enough of letting that voice drowning out all the good things she knew about herself, all the wonderful things that Baba and Guido had pointed out about her, again and again.

She'd spent most of her teens playing second fiddle to her half sister, Nadia, always falling into her shadow, always being measured against Mama and Nadia's beauty, and coming up short. After losing Baba, she'd buried herself in her studies, in looking after Guido and Paloma. She'd never indulged in the simple pleasure of putting on a pretty dress, doing her hair, using a flick of lip gloss so that her wide mouth shimmered invitingly. She'd never primped herself, wanting to catch a man's gaze, never seen herself as an object of desire.

She did all these things now, and she did them with Sebastian's gray gaze and wicked smile in mind. It was the simplest of thrills and yet, she'd never experienced it before him. Never felt the need at all.

It was a new freedom from her fears that had tethered her for so long, a new identity even, as more than the brainy freak, the crow in the cuckoo nest, more than a caregiver for her sons and others.

As she pushed her feet into designer flip-flops, there was a zing in her belly, a pep to her step. She walked down to the beach, feeling not only carefree and relaxed for the first time in ages, but with anticipation throbbing through every inch of her. For the evening ahead and for the future.

CHAPTER NINE

WHEN SHE FINALLY found Sebastian—much farther along the private strip of beach than she usually traversed with the boys—it was to find him staring at the sky with a grim set to his mouth. She'd rarely seen him in such a somber mood that Laila felt her curiosity increase a thousand times over.

Without disturbing him, she kicked off her sandals and scrunched her feet into the glorious-feeling sand. The sand was still warm from the hot day but the waves lapping at her felt icily cold. A childish giggle escaped her as she let the water barely touch her toes before running back. With the tide coming in faster and rougher, she felt that little lurch in her belly when the water pulled away the sand from right under her feet. Kind of how her life felt at the moment. And yet, she wanted to be here, with this man. So much for calculating her risks.

For a while, she played her game with the waves, more than content to wait out his dark mood. *A partnership,* she'd told Thea, and now she realized she'd meant it. But it had to be for more than just the boys. It had to be for them. And she was already invested deep enough to know that Sebastian fascinated her, in more than one way. It had been so from the first time she'd set her eyes and her plans on him.

Finally, she felt his attention move to her, as real as if he'd run those rough artist's hands over her skin. Like she had tiny little antennae wired specifically for his attention.

"If you have come here hoping to mellow my mood, you'll fail," he said in that soft voice he wielded as a weapon. Or was it a shield? she wondered with a fresh perspective relatively free of her own insecurities. "Unless you will let me take you on the sand…" His white teeth gleamed against his olive skin like a predator's warning. "That might mellow me down."

"Why would I want to mellow you at all, Sebastian? It is rare enough that you show your true colors. And as for taking me roughly in the sand—" her breath hitched in her throat at the image that came "—you're just being a tease. Sand or bed or wall or the pristine marble floor of my bedroom, I'm yours for the taking."

His rough curse added to the symphony of the waves.

"Is another migraine coming on?" she ventured, eager to know.

He shook his head, dislodging a lock of hair onto his forehead. "Is that why you came running?"

"Wow, you're like a prickly bull right now, huh?"

"So, you should run away screaming, Dr. Jaafri."

"I think I'll stay right here."

He shrugged, without quite meeting her eyes.

"You were hard on Alexandros the other day."

Another curse. "Of all the things to bring up… Why are we talking about my infernal brother?"

"Because I have a point to make."

"You know he does not like you."

"Of course I know he doesn't like me and that's a cheap shot," Laila said, scrunching her nose. "Alexandros likes control in all things, yes? And the fact that I will not fall into line or that you are not taking enough actions to make me fall in line, and all of this is causing too many unknowns when all he wants is quiet and comfort for Annika…does not sit with him well."

Sebastian turned to face her and admiration glinted in his eyes. "Anything more?"

"In his mind, I'm also the reason for the strife between him and Annika. Right now, I make a convenient target for him to blame, among all the unknowns."

Sebastian grinned, those thin lines fanning out from the edges of his eyes again. She loved when he smiled like that, with real mirth, without mockery. There was already a catalog of the wide variety of his smiles in her head.

"And yet you *scold* me that I'm hard on him?"

"I'm not scolding you."

"You have that stern voice you use with the boys. For all the indulging you do, that voice means business. Although, I would be up for experimenting with that voice in bed, just so you know," he said, nudging her shoulder with his.

Heat streaked through her lower belly and Laila had to retrace her thoughts. "Promises and threats, *Kyrios Skalas*," she said, taunting him.

The moment stretched between them, full of sparks and longing and…heated desire.

“What else have you surmised of my brother?”

“His dislike of me is mostly based on something other than logic. When he discovers that, it will go away. As long as he does not extend it to Nikos and Zayn—which he hasn’t—I do not care if he approves of me or not.”

“You sound very used to being disliked, Dr. Jaafri,” he said, shocking her with his perception.

“Nobody gets used to being disliked, do they?” She laughed to bury the pain in her words, but it came out sounding hollow. But then, she had almost no pretensions when it came to Sebastian. So why start now? “Nobody should have to get used to being mocked for being odd or unconventional or differently wired or being sensitive. It’s especially cruel when it comes…from people who should protect you,” she said softly, acknowledging something she hadn’t until now. “I’m used to it. But I’ll do everything in my power to protect Zayn from something like that.”

“He has to face the world on his own merit, too, Laila. Or he would never know what he was capable of.”

Laila heard the almost mournful note in that and tried not to wonder what would make this seemingly powerful man sound so. The thought was terrifying even in her head. “Yes, well, that’s why we both are needed, no? You can push them toward being their own selves and I can coddle them just a little.”

Apparently, all it took to mellow Sebastian’s dark mood was talking about them as a team. She could almost feel him put on the easy, casual mask as he replied, “Fine. Let’s talk about the mighty Alexandros Skalas and why you think I hurt him.”

"It comes to you naturally…being a nurturer. Which is rare enough in powerful men who're used to getting what they want. Maybe it's because you were used to Annika as a kid or maybe it's your artistic nature that pushes you to see the purity of spirit in children, I don't know," she said, clearly probing. "But it does not come easily to Alexandros, and it is also clear that the idea of being a parent terrifies him. And yet, instead of offering him some kind of comfort, you rubbed it in his face. I would say it was quite cruel of you, but luckily for me and the boys, I know that you don't have a cruel bone in your body."

"It would be dangerous to put so much trust in me, Laila."

"That's a one-eighty if I've ever heard one," she said, not heeding the very real warning in his words.

He tucked his hands into the pockets of his trousers and examined her, as if gauging her worthiness. Laila stood her ground. After a while, he exhaled and spoke. "This is the first time in our lives that I'm better at something than him. And it is a big thing, given it's a child, and his child tomorrow, that we're talking about. Alexandros is used to being perfect at everything. Except this is not a skill set you acquire overnight, is it?"

Laila slapped his arm. "That's what I'm talking about. You're…enjoying his misery. That's…awful, Sebastian."

"Well, he was good at everything growing up. The perfect heir, the well-behaved son and a genius whiz kid with numbers and stocks… For a banking dynasty's heir, that's like knowing how to alchemize everything into gold."

Her breath suspended in her throat as she got a tiny glimpse into what made Sebastian so different and so… unpredictable. "And you?" she asked, terrified of being shunted behind that invisible circle he drew around himself.

"I failed at everything he excelled at, and anything I was supposed to be good at. I got expelled out of every private school in Europe, so Alexandros had to return home, too. I made my tutors' life hell until they ran away screaming. I complained of constant headaches and visions and was high maintenance until I found something to calm me down in my teens. I drew endless amounts of art that no one could make head or tail of. Konstantin loathed my very existence, so I gave him more reasons to do so by failing at everything he set me to do."

"Your father?" Laila whispered, anxious to know more of what had made him and terrified of what it might be.

"Yes, the great Konstantin Skalas who was full of rot on the inside. He…did his best to mold me into another version of Alexandros. Because one paragon of a son wasn't enough for the egotistical control freak. The more he tried, the more I loathed it, and the more I acted out. He didn't miss a single chance to use his words and his fists against me."

Laila couldn't breathe. And when she spoke, her words were fragile, insubstantial, full of rage against this…monster of a man who would terrorize a defenseless child. Suddenly, so many things about Sebastian became clear. "What about your grandmother? And your mother? Why didn't they protect you?"

"Thea didn't know for a long time. And my mother... He'd already terrified her until she was afraid of her own shadow and lost herself in drink."

Laila felt a surge of anger toward the woman but tempered it from turning it into judgment. But the thought of no one aiding a young Sebastian, of perverting his sense of self...made her want to rage out. Somehow, she managed to sound steady. "I'm... I have no words, Sebastian. I see where your fierceness for the boys comes from. You're..." Another realization struck her. "So, you have spent your entire life shaming the Skalas name as some sort of revenge?"

He shrugged, his smile grim. "The need to dirty the name became far too entrenched in me by the time Alexandros discovered Konstantin's treatment of me. And when he did... He did his best to shield me, begged me not to fuel Konstantin's rages. For the next few years, Alexandros planned and schemed and strategized with Thea to bring Konstantin under his heel and then he ousted him from the bank and our lives."

"You resent him for saving you?" Laila bit out, before she could phrase it better.

"Alexandros did not save me," he said, a jagged edge to his answer that forbade her to probe more.

But something lingered just out of her reach and Laila couldn't quite catch what it was. "So, because he was better than you as a child, you will rub this fear of his in his face?" she said instead.

He turned toward her, finally paying full attention to her windblown hair and her new dress and her pink lips. Something hot came awake in his eyes.

He rubbed a hand over his tired face. “I reacted out of instinct. Although I do not want him to terrify my sons with his ugly face.”

When she gasped, he raised his brows and grinned. Moving close suddenly, he caught one stray corkscrew curl and pulled it until it stood straight in his fingers.

Laila let him tug her closer, thick clumps of her curls between his fingers as leverage. Her scalp prickled, the remembered sensation of those fingers delving deep and driving her wild acute. “He needs you, Sebastian.”

He scoffed. “Annika didn’t tell him about the boys before she could tell me… He doesn’t have to throw a tantrum about it.”

Laila pressed her forehead into his chest, smiling at the thread of stubborn pride in his voice. “That’s not what he cares about.”

“No? Because Alexandros doesn’t have a whole range of emotional breadth.”

And you do? she wanted to ask but she knew the answer. Every day, every little action of his showed her what a complicated, complex man Sebastian was. And with each moment, her draw to him became stronger, nearly irresistible, as if he was a whole gravitational field unto himself and she had no choice but to be pulled into his orbit. But she wanted more than just to circle him endlessly.

She wanted a collision, an explosion, she wanted to reach his raw, burning center. Because she was almost sure that beneath all the masks, Sebastian hid his true self—a man who had to fight every day since he was a child to be himself. Just like her, but in much more horrible circumstances. Was that why nothing and no one was sacred to him? Why he moved through life the way he did?

Suddenly, whatever it was that he wanted from Guido took a new shape, an all-new dimension. She'd never wondered what a powerful, charismatic man like him could want from a poor, old man like Guido.

"Don't leave me hanging now, Dr. Jaafri," he said, watching her closely.

Laila somehow found her words, even as her mind mined for reasons. "Alexandros is angry with Annika that she upset herself over keeping it secret from you. And he's angry with you that you won't let it go. Which means he finds it impossible to confide in you that he's irrationally terrified that he might not be a great father, especially in comparison to you."

Sebastian released her hair and it popped back into its usual curls. He cupped her cheek in his rough hand, tilting her chin up to meet his eyes. "He's not terrified. My brother has never been scared of anything and he…"

"He is *now*. That's why he freezes around Nikos and Zayn."

A corded arm went around her waist and pulled her, until her breasts flattened against his chest in delicious torment. "Why do you care so much about him?"

There was almost a note of childish peevishness to it and Laila smothered a smile. "Why does it bother you so much that Annika didn't tell you about the boys when you know deep in your heart that she did the right thing?"

"Because she owed her loyalty to me at that point. Not to you."

"Is that all?" Laila pushed, pressing her cheek to his chest, seeking the kind of real intimacy that he might not allow but wanting it anyway. Slowly, she was beginning to see through his mask. Sex and seduction and sinful bets were easy for him, even shields to keep the world at bay. True communication about his needs, showing his real self to the world or caring about anything, not so much.

His heart thundered against her ear as he held her loosely, humoring her, she was sure. He was so…solid and real around her that she couldn't believe she wasn't dreaming. Only her dreams had grown bigger and more improbable since she'd arrived here.

His silence told her she'd been right about his anger toward Annika. Lifting her head, she rubbed her forehead against his stubbled chin. "I care about both of them. Annika and your brother." She had even more respect for Alexandros for taking Sebastian's side when he'd been no more an adult himself, but she was wise enough to not probe a festering wound. "She's been a good friend to me, even though I approached her with my own agenda. She spent hours reassuring me that this was right. She took a huge risk by not telling you. I've not had someone like that in my corner in a long time." She blinked away the sudden tears the thought brought to her throat. "And you…won't even look at her. Please… forgive her. Forgive her so that she's not upset anymore, so that they're not at odds with each other."

Now both his arms were around her waist, and he

dipped low enough for her to feel his warm breath on her lips.

"You're a dangerous woman, Dr. Jaafri," he said, his gaze moving over every inch of her as if he meant to unlock her, piece by piece.

"I'm not, really," she said, laughing at the very prospect. "In fact, I'm terribly easy to see through once you figure out the key to me."

"Maybe the danger, then, is in my perception of you," he said, his mouth curving but the smile not quite reaching his eyes.

She frowned. "Then that would make you like every other man who called me too brainy and too competitive and too logical, leaving very little femininity behind."

His rough hand circled her nape in a hold that had dampness blooming at her core. "No one is all of one thing, *pethi mou*. Maybe you're all of those things and there is no shame in them. But I see more to you, too, and that's what makes you so…irresistible."

It was impossible to not believe him, especially when his body was radiating the same tension she felt.

He bent down and licked the shell of her ear before he said, "I'll talk to Ani tomorrow and I'll teach Alexandros how to not freeze like a deer in the headlights around his nephews. For you."

Laila slapped his chest. "For me? *Please.* You adore her. Stop making this—"

His arm tightened like a vise around her, and she loved the little cage he built. Loved the rub and slide of her curves against his hardness. "Accept that this is one of your wishes I'm granting."

"No way am I using up one of those on something you were already going to do."

"Now who's cheating?" he demanded, his mouth running a heated trail down her neck.

"Not me," she said, shivering. "Wait, I do have a question. If you answer it, then I'll admit that you've granted me another wish."

He licked at her pulse and breathed the question into her skin. "Ask me."

"Tell me about your migraines."

And why you hide your art, she wanted to say. But there was only so much risk or rejection she could expose herself to at a given time.

"Not much to tell. I have had them for as long as I can remember. Mama used to keep me close to her because I would roar and yell and scream when I was in throes of it. Konstantin thought they made me weak, called me a runt. Would make me run laps around the estate after I recovered as if to make up for them."

"They continue to this day?"

"I have seen specialists all around the world. They don't know what to make of it and I have learned to live with them."

"But—"

He didn't allow her to say more, capturing her mouth with his. His lips were soft and seeking, as if he was searching for something only she could give. Laila sank into the kiss, stunned at how much he seemed to need the gentle tasting as much as she did. It was a soft landing, a subtle invitation to surrender without asking, a sweet promise that he would never hurt her.

When he released her, she mewled like a cat, and buried her face in his throat. She didn't feel shy so much as protective about all these new feelings the kiss evoked. Some magical wildness in Sebastian offered both safety and excitement and she thought she might spend her whole life happily swinging between those opposing points.

"I thought you would ask me something for yourself." Desire made his words low, rough-sounding. "To get Alexandros off your delicious ass with all that stuff."

She shrugged and raised her head. "He's only doing what's right for all of us, no?"

"It is a lot to get used to," he said, nibbling at her lips. "But you don't complain. You never complain. You're a puzzle, Dr. Jaafri, one I intend to crack."

"How many more wishes do I have left, Mr. Skalas?"

"One more, *yineka mou*," he said, that roguish grin back in his eyes.

"You're so sure of getting your way, aren't you?"

"Always," he said, his fingers playing at the nape of her neck.

"Is that why you won't give us both what we want?"

A fake gasp escaped those near-perfect lips. "I'm saving myself for marriage, Dr. Jaafri. How dare you try to corrupt me with your swaying hips and sexy smiles?"

She laughed, even as she was aware that he wasn't really answering her question. It was hard to concentrate on thoughts when his hands were stroking all over her, and his mouth was nibbling at her neck. "Then I would like to grant you a wish, too."

His head jerked up, almost hitting her. Surprise

made his lush lower lip slacken for a moment. "Why such generosity?"

"For being you, Sebastian." When his big body stilled around her, she added, "And okay, maybe to mellow you down a bit."

He tucked a curl away from her face with a tenderness she didn't miss. Or the sudden gravelly tenor to his words when he spoke. "And what would you grant me?"

"I want to make you lose your mind. Here, now," she said, looking around as if she could spot any rogue cameras. "Give you new memories around this place."

He cursed and grinned, though she had a feeling it was a filter hiding his true emotion. Then his teeth dug into that sensuous lower lip. "You're on. Only if you join me."

Heat streaked her cheeks and Laila instantly felt her nipples peak to attention. She rubbed her thighs, tempted beyond good sense. "I don't want to be caught by any cameras."

"And if I want us to be caught on camera? If I want more adventure and more boldness and less inhibition from my lover?" he asked, still smiling. But there was a hard, lethal edge to it as if he meant to test her limits or her trust or to assuage his own need for something.

With any other man, Laila would have backed down from the explicit gauntlet thrown down, because it would have been to expose her fears, to mock her "frigidity." But with Sebastian, she thrilled in his asking, that he would give her a chance to be what he wanted. To meet him as his equal, in this, she needed it as she needed air.

"Then I suggest you give me some time and a bit of a

private location for my first time on camera and then I'll try to get into it," she said, bluffing her way to a boldness she loved within herself. "The last thing we want is to shock your very traditional grandmother with my naked ass rolling around in the sand."

He laughed and kissed her hard enough to steal her breath away. His fingers gripped the back of her head as he devoured her mouth with firm, hungry strokes, as if he was afraid she might vanish. Rough and soft, his mouth and his stubbled jaw were a contrast in pleasure and delicious pain. When he pulled back, they were both breathing hard, and his eyes carried a wild light that was different from his usual bored charm. "You're an unending delight. Though I would only want what you want, Dr. Jaafri."

"Right now, I want a little cover from the villa."

"Your genie awaits, then."

Anticipation throbbed within her as he pulled her in the opposite direction of the villa. Running on the slipping sand, with waves lapping at her feet, with her hand tucked into his, Laila felt this…figment of joy like she'd never tasted before. It was in the back of her throat, in her chest, in her belly, in all of her, like a warm pulse. And she wanted to hang on to it, nurture it until it became a living flame that would suffuse her entire being.

Shockingly enough, Sebastian brought her to a large outhouse-type structure almost half a mile along the beach, with lots of glass walls and a high roof, answering another question that had been eating away at her. It was a recluse artist's painting cabin, Laila thought, staring eagerly at what lay beyond the small entry area where there were a bunch of unused easels and various shelves with pots of paint.

"This is your space," she said inanely.

A grunt was his answer.

Her curiosity lasted a bare second as Sebastian cupped her face with both hands and kissed her senseless. There was something new in how he kissed her, his hands roving over her body, his large, lean frame caging her against the glass wall. "You wore this dress for me?" he said, licking into her mouth.

"I wanted to corrupt you just a little," she whispered, clinging to his mouth.

When he reached for the threads of her dress strings at her nape, Laila patted his hand away. "This is my show," she said, feeling his gaze on her skin like a laser beam of want and heat. "Hands in the air, please."

He grabbed onto the beam above him, his lean hips thrusting forward in a "do your worst" pose, and she thought she might just die from the decadent sight he made. Reaching him, she unbuttoned his linen shirt—full of paint splotches—and then pushed it off his broad shoulders. If she hadn't been completely bamboozled by the man's sex appeal three years ago, she'd have noticed that he didn't have a wastrel playboy's body, or face or hands. He was all raw, rough masculinity, a man who used his body both as a weapon and a shield.

Leaning down, she pressed a trail of kisses down his chest and licked the slab of thick abdominal muscles as if he was her very own ice cream cone.

His hands went into her hair, sinking deep to hold her still. "Is this allowed, Dr. Jaafri?"

"Yes," she said, breathing it into his taut skin. Then she dragged her teeth over the same trail, marking him.

Then she undid his pants and snuck her hand in to cradle his shaft. God above, he was so hard, and he was all hers. She bit her lower lip as she fisted his erection, remembering the feel of him moving inside her. "Tell me what you like. Show me how to make this so good that you're as desperate for me as I'm for you."

Head thrown back, muscles bunched in his neck, he was all harsh masculine beauty that even her logical mind glitched. A rough grunt fell from his mouth as she rubbed a thumb over the soft head. "Squeeze harder. Move your fist up and down."

Laila complied and soon, he was thrusting his hips into her hand, in a sinuous dance *she* was leading, and she'd never felt more feminine, more in touch with her own wild cravings, just more…alive. And she wanted more. With her other hand, she pushed his pants farther down, before sinking to her knees.

She felt his shock in his stillness, rather than heard it. Pupils blown, breathing ragged, he looked…like one of those sculptures by some great Renaissance artist. And yet, Sebastian was gloriously alive, able to feel the full spectrum of emotions unlike any other man she had ever met.

"You don't have to do this, Laila," he said, a ragged edge to his tone that said how much he did want it.

"Have you known me to do anything that I'm not into, Sebastian?" she said, teasing him with firm strokes. And then she licked the thick head experimentally. "Tell me, Sebastian. You promised you'd grant me this."

"Why?"

"Because I want the knowledge that I broke your control."

"You do it every day as you smile at me over the breakfast table with our sons in between us, *agapi mou*."

Her breath hung in her throat as she wondered if she read more meaning into those guttural words. "I want your pleasure at my hands, and your ruin, too. For making me think I was party to cheating. For making me guilty for reliving that night. For..."

For giving her what she hadn't known she needed, she finished to herself.

He smiled and Laila knew he understood this compulsive need to push past any previous limits with each other. To earn surrender in new ways. That he was here with her, and not just the convenient mother of his sons.

His fingers sank back into her curls and gripped the back of her head with a possessiveness she reveled in. Who knew sex could be so fun and primal and...raw?

"Open your mouth wide and take me in. Tap my thigh if it's too much. And remember, *agapi*, breathe through it."

Laila followed his instructions and soon, he had her how he needed her. She heard his pithy grunts and his filthy curses and his ragged breaths and instinctive thrusts. When she stole a look at him, she saw this painfully beautiful, increasingly complex man rendered in strokes of stark need. And seeing him like this...was as arousing as it was revealing, for it destroyed all the lies she'd told herself about relationships and romance and sex and…love. Lies she'd spun about why she'd surrendered so easily to him three years ago.

It made her realize that at heart she was very much a simple woman with simple desires, that she'd hid behind formulae and calculations and models, that she'd buried to feel right within how she was built and thought. And somehow, Sebastian was the key to unlocking it all and there was no end to all the things she wanted to experience with him, that she wanted to make him feel.

Tears smarted when he went deep with one long stroke and breath was a mirage. Her knees felt the hardness of the rough floor, her cheeks the burn. Laila dug her hands into his thighs and doubled down. The sound of his shaft hitting the roof of her mouth was so erotically filthy that it made her core drip with need. Then he was pulling out of her mouth, and her to her feet, which were barely steady. Before she could protest the abrupt non-finish, he was kissing her, one hand sneaking under her neckline and tweaking her aching nipple.

"Come over with me," he said, rough fingers pulling the hem of her dress up over her thighs, delving deep into her folds with a gentleness that might break her. Then he hooked one finger inside her, hitting that perfect spot, and Laila thought she might be seeing stars. "*Cristos*, you're so…responsive."

They came together like that, watching each other, stroking each other, chasing each other's pleasure. Laila dug her teeth into his bicep as her climax ripped through her, turning her limbs into liquid sensation, and felt the hot lash of his climax on her belly. His satisfied grunt was a sound she wanted to hear again and again. Breath seesawing out of her mouth, she fell onto him—damp and sweaty—while he wiped her belly with the edges of his shirt.

"Are you well, Dr. Jaafri?"

The tenderness of his question made Laila swallow.

She heard a distinct ringing in her ears, which was probably her heart trying to pound out of her body because she was…so in love with this man who held her as if she was fragile and precious. The realization moved through her in far-flung ripples, turning her inside out, making her feel both new and entrenched in her own skin.

Feeling vulnerable, she tried to pull away from him, but her legs gave out from under her like a newborn fawn's. With a tenderness she suddenly, desperately wished was real, he gathered her and pulled her higher against his solid warmth. A tear ran out of the corner of her eye, and she wiped at it roughly, wishing her body didn't betray her so easily.

"I'm sorry. I don't know what's happening," she said, still battling the sudden realization.

"Shh… There's no need for words when it comes to this between us," he said, rubbing his cheek against hers. "Except praise for me for sending you to outer space."

She chuckled, but it was slight and watery, and she kept her eyes closed, wondering what he would see if she let him. He kissed her temple and then her cheek and then the corner of her mouth. "It's okay, Laila."

He'd said that before, too, infinitely patient, and so ready to grant her whatever she asked for.

God, how had she allowed this? How could she love

him with this wild abandon she'd never known before? What if he tired of her while this new…emotion flickered in her chest like a live flame? What if she agreed to marry him and they were locked in a convenient, sterile marriage for the rest of their lives? Could she bear to be near him and know he might never want her for the right reasons? What was the shape of her life if she always just stayed a means for him to fulfill what he'd been denied as a child?

The more she learned of his childhood, the more Laila was sure that Sebastian had never cared about anything much, had never been given the chance to. His art and his sons were now the only things that mattered to him. What if he just didn't have the ability to care about her like she did him?

"You're still trembling," he said, tightening his arms around her.

"You rocked my world," she said, striving for a flirty tone that had never come easy even before this. So she gave in to the only avenue open to her, to feel and show this new emotion. Opening her mouth, she tasted his skin, bit into the hard muscle of his shoulder. "You never told me what had you in such a foul mood."

He was quiet for so long that she resigned herself to his silence, to the fact that there was only so much she could demand, that soon she was going to come up on his hard limits.

With a rough exhale, she tried to pull back when he said, "This…painting I'm working on…" He cleared his throat, his words sounding like they came from some far-off place in him that he never went to in front of others. Laila instinctively knew that he wasn't used to talking about this, that he was letting her enter a forbidden place in his head. "It won't come together. It's the one thing in my goddamned life I've always been good at and the one thing that…calms that noise in my head. But for some reason, this one won't come together the way I see it in my head. I hate it. And I…hate feeling like my canvas won't speak to me when it is the only thing that has always known me."

The real, unfiltered, unmasked Sebastian Skalas…

Laila nodded wordlessly, tears prickling behind her eyelids, and tightened her arms around his waist, hoping he wouldn't push her away. She didn't understand why he didn't let the world see who he was or what peace he gained by hiding himself away—even from himself, she was beginning to realize. But she felt his pain and his powerlessness as if it were her own and she loved him a little more for giving her a tiny bit more than he wanted to, clearly.

She clung to him for long moments, knowing all she had were trite words to take on what she was realizing was a lifetime's pain, so she just held him and he let her and it was enough as darkness fell around them.

CHAPTER TEN

Days after Laila had driven him wild and ravenous with her words and her mouth in the very place where he had never brought another soul to, Sebastian was still feeling unsettled. That encounter had been replaying in his head like a loop, for more than one reason.

Laila with her wild hair and generous promises, granting him a wish.

Laila, who made it easy to talk about things he'd never talked to another soul about—not even his twin.

Laila with her roving mouth all over his chest.

Laila on her knees looking up at him with those big eyes and those dark cherry-colored lips.

Laila holding his gaze with a tender, possessive hunger as her soft hand stroked him to dizzying heights of pleasure.

Laila who clung to him, trembling, and shaking, hiding none of her vulnerability.

He'd never looked a lover in the eye like that, at the throes of release. Never had been pushed off the edge because of the look in a woman's eye. Never needed to hold the woman after, a little flicker of dread and a host of other emotions rooting him in place.

It was as if Laila was the genie with all the magic and she had sprinkled it all over him, alchemizing sex into something else. For the first time in his life, he'd been left with a niggling sense of loss he'd never known before, even as his body felt fully satiated. Usually, it was all he could do to get away from his partner when he'd satisfied them both. With Laila, he had been glad that she'd clung to him because he hadn't been ready to let go of her, either.

Now he wondered if it was all so different with her because when he saw her, he saw his sons' faces first. Saw Nikos's grin and Zayn's considering stare in her features. Saw the means to the deepest wish he'd indulged in as a child who would never have his father's approval.

With a desperation that kept clawing at him every moment now, he wanted all those reasons to be true. He needed them to be true. He needed Laila to mean nothing but a means to the end.

All of it rang untrue and hollow to his own ears.

Was it the childhood shame he had shared with her? Was that why he suddenly felt raw and vulnerable around her?

He had always told himself that the shame was Konstantin's—to terrify an innocent child, not his. But he had never gone into such detail with anyone else, not even his twin. And Alexandros knew everything. For all he'd never given it voice, raking over it with her had felt cleansing rather than poking a festering wound. Like giving her the blurry, torn map to his soul.

He had spent years developing awareness and control of his roiling emotions, right from adolescence—no one was going to help him with it, and yet, now his chest felt like it was a tangle of knotted wires, pricking and poking at his conscience. Like he'd meant to paint one thing on the canvas and something else was taking shape.

Like his heart wanted, no, needed, things beyond the boundaries he'd drawn around it a long time ago. Like it craved things it didn't know how to feel and give, things it was wholly unworthy of.

There was another strange thing happening to him. But this one he didn't fight. Didn't resist. He'd been spooked enough by what had happened between him and Laila that he had gone back to his art that very night. While it had fought him for almost a month, driving him near feral, suddenly it poured through his fingers with such frenzy that he'd spent every free minute working on his painting. Despite the thing that was emerging on the canvas, it was the one thing still under his control.

But he might as well have not tried to avoid her while he untangled himself, because Laila was doing it all the same. Something about that evening had spooked her. He felt her eyes on him as always, devouring him and seeking something in turn, the easy camaraderie and partnership they had developed over almost three months was gone. There was a wary look in her eyes as if she knew now what he was up to, as if she didn't dare come close again. But desire and heat thrummed between them, arcing over with just one look, one errant touch.

"Sebastian?" Ani said, stretching her hand out to him from the grass. They were all playing in the huge meadow behind the villa that sunny afternoon. The perfect picnic spot Laila had chosen for the boys with a blanket and snacks and toys. Giant, gnarled trees that he'd once hidden behind offered spots of shade to his sons now.

Giving her his hand, Sebastian pulled his sister-in-law up and then steadied her with a laugh as she wobbled on her feet. "Thank you," he whispered and then kissed her cheek, knowing that even in this, Laila had been spot-on.

He hadn't really been angry with Annika—he'd just given the fear inside him that label.

Without meeting his eyes, Ani wrapped her arms around his waist, like she used to when she'd been a little girl, following him across this very meadow, forever dogging his steps, making his days a little lighter.

He wrapped his arms around her, unable to meet her eyes. Now, all these years later, she'd given Laila enough confidence to tell him the truth. He thought he must have done one thing right.

Ani raised those large eyes of hers, shimmering with tears, to his face finally. "Xander won't come out and ask, as he's still upset with you. Or maybe he worries that you won't accept."

"Ask me what?" Sebastian said, frowning.

"Will you be her godfather?" Annika said, putting her palm on her belly.

Awed and ashamed at once, he could only nod.

Ani wiped the tears from her cheeks, gave him a watery smile, grabbed one of the toy water guns and jumped into the fray with the boys. Though Zayn was no less reserved with her than he was with everyone else, he had taken to calling her *Ani Auntie*, sitting close when she played the cello—clearly it soothed him—and following her around with those big eyes full of curiosity. Used to roughhousing with her own three brothers, Ani knew exactly how to engage the boys' attention.

And now to be godfather to her and Alexandros's daughter… Sebastian felt as if his cup was overflowing with all the good things he'd once desperately wanted. Needed. His wildest dreams as a child come true. Except, nothing of the innocence of that child was left in him. He might not be a monster like Konstantin, but he was beginning to wonder what his real self was under the smoke and mirrors.

His gaze shifted to Laila, who was on her knees, fixing a stuck toy gun for Nikos. The sun caught the golden highlights in her hair, made the smooth skin of her neck and bare arms glimmer like burnished gold. Her sleeveless silk top was wet after the boys had caught her with their sprays and stuck to her skin, outlining her small breasts.

Just the sight of her filled Sebastian with hunger and…something he hadn't known the taste of in years. Or never, even. And it was the newness of this thing inside him, when he'd thought he'd glutted himself on all the riches and excess in the world, that had him so out of balance.

As if aware of his perusal, Laila looked up. Emotion he couldn't name flashed through her eyes before she offered him the polite smile of the last week. He felt the overwhelming urge to pick her up, throw her over his shoulder and carry her away and kiss that wariness and doubt out of her. He'd seduce her until she agreed to marry him and this…new furor and uncertainty in his head would die down. Wouldn't it? Once he had her bound to him, what was left to worry about?

Instead, he walked back to where his grandmother was sitting, his muscles burning with the need for action.

Alexandros stood against one of the large trees, his stance rigid, watching his wife. Annika was chasing Nikos, her cheeks reddish brown in the sun, her long braid already half wet.

"Thank you for letting it go," said Alexandros, his jaw tight. Sebastian heard the emotion that his twin rarely let anyone other than his wife see. "I haven't seen her laugh like that in a while. But instead of begging you to forgive her, I've been demanding that she let this grief over you go, demanding that she be well for my sake. Even after three years, I want to control everything around her so that she isn't hurt, so that she is happy." He thrust a rough hand through his hair, a scoff escaping his mouth. "I still haven't learned it enough that to love her means to let her be who she is, and to live with this…discomfort. And I have to do it all over again with a tiny little girl who will…be my responsibility."

So that was at the root of his twin's fear—not that he wouldn't care about his daughter but that he would do it wrong because he loved her so much already.

The angst in his words made shame burn through Sebastian's chest. It had been childish and selfish of him to continue his stubborn silence against Annika.

Only the past few days, with Laila's thoughts in his head, had he been able to understand that Ani had become a convenient target for him to blame for his own actions.

His anger toward her was a shield to avoid facing the fact that he might not have ever known about his sons because of how he had almost ruined an old man. Only now, did he see shades of Konstantin in his own actions—the ruthlessness with which he had gone after Guido. He'd justified luring the old man into gambling debt, betting his little home until he lost it to Sebastian, because he'd spent most of his adult life looking for his mother, another victim of Konstantin.

But the price would have been high if Laila hadn't taken a chance on him, despite his actions. If whatever sense of ethics she possessed hadn't driven her to seek him out. He would have lost this present, this future, by his own actions.

"Laila made me see I was causing too much strife between you both. That I was hard on you the other day."

Alexandros turned, his face slack with surprise. "Your instincts were right about her. You knew about my…feelings for Ani long before I did, too."

"Trust that feeling, Alexandros. When your daughter is here, that feeling will guide you, too."

His brother gave another nod and then a bark of a laugh. "You have always been a better man than I am."

"I fought Konstantin so hard to be myself," Sebastian said, betraying his turmoil.

"And you have succeeded. You're a world-renowned artist. Your earliest paintings are coveted even now, go for millions in auctions. You spat in our father's face for how he mocked your art, you showed him false by becoming a man in your own right without the aid of the Skalas name, without touching your legacy. And I… I've never asked why you don't tell the world who you truly are. I've never asked you to share your art with me. But Sebastian…" Alexandros turned toward him, and until this moment, Sebastian hadn't realized how perceptive his twin could be when it came to him.

After all, they'd been each other's mirror in so many ways and witness to each other's best and worst.

"What?" he demanded, sick of the dread in his stomach.

"You have been a good man, Sebastian. Until now, at least."

"And what does that mean?" he said belligerently, hating that Alexandros was speaking the same doubts he already had himself.

"Being in love with a woman like Ani… It has changed what I can see, Sebastian." His twin gave a nod toward Laila, who was squealing and laughing and running up the meadow with their sons chasing her. "Does she know that you're stalking her like a predator does its prey? That you're not interested in—?"

"She came to me. She told me what her needs are," Sebastian said, cutting off what his twin would recklessly give voice to. "I'm simply showing her what the future could be between us."

"You're just playing along, to seduce her to your way. Making a show of giving her everything."

"*I am* giving her everything she asks for and it so happens that we agree on most important things. Why is taking advantage of that wrong?"

"It's…duplicitous, because you're doing it with a goal in sight."

"And here I thought you would champion me for making this right."

"Right for whom, though?" Alexandros said, sounding more frustrated on his behalf than Sebastian had ever heard him. "Maybe, finally, I see that some risks or gambles are not just worth it, that some things are sacred. I thought you knew that, Sebastian. I thought you understood better than me that the cost is too high."

"What aren't you saying, Alexandros?"

"Either you're lying to her or to yourself. And all these lies…will crash down on you when it's too late."

Sebastian stood there, long after Alexandros deserted him to join the noisy melee. He laughed when Nikos aimed at his uncle and then took off on his chubby legs and Alexandros made a show of not being able to catch him. He smiled when Zayn followed his twin and his uncle and auntie at an appropriate distance.

He felt his heart thud when Laila slipped and fell, and Alexandros gave her his hand and pulled her up, dusted her shoulder off and kissed her cheek and he could see the twinkle of joy in her eyes from all the way over here.

He froze when Laila's amber gaze sought him across the meadow and she gave him a small nod, and mouthed thank you, for fixing *his problem* with his brother and sister-in-law.

He fought the instinct to chase her across the meadow and demand that she give him surrender. He fought the pull she had on him but refused to give up his goal.

His twin's warning resonated like a painful gong, especially since it was exactly what he'd been dwelling on. He had never meant to hurt Laila and yet, suddenly it felt like all he was doing was pulling the worst kind of deception over her. But neither could he explore the other option. He could not let himself…feel. Not when, to this day, he hadn't recovered from his mother's leaving, when it felt like a necessary part of him was missing.

Not when he couldn't risk putting himself out there again. Which left him with only one choice.

He would bury this doubt, this new…weakness and continue with his plan to persuade Laila to marry him. Maybe then, all this vague dread would disappear. Maybe when he had her legally bound to him, when he knew that she was his, it would all fall into place.

CHAPTER ELEVEN

LAILA HAD ENJOYED a couple of more weeks of what she considered a happy, relatively functioning, well-adjusted time with her sons' new family when it all came to an end. Not to mention that her academic paper had been accepted and she had a chance to present it a conference in a few weeks. Everything was going right or everything was going wrong and she didn't know what was what.

She and Sebastian hadn't kissed or touched or…exchanged anything more than a look since her realization. They seemed to have settled into some kind of holding pattern, bracing against the next upcoming turn in their nonrelationship relationship. She knew why she'd pulled back.

While the realization that she loved him only grew stronger, as if planting roots deep within her very soul, it also spurred hope and fear equally. She was afraid she would blurt it all out to him if he so much as he looked at her for too long and she didn't how to build defenses against his reaction.

If he laughed at her, or mocked her…she would fall apart. And she was cowardly enough to know she didn't want to lose his respect, or be seen as pathetic, cowardly enough to continue in this holding pattern, to lie to herself that he was preoccupied with his art.

He'd even fixed his fight with Ani and Alexandros. He'd been communicating more with her about his moods and work habits, though it felt more like ticking off a checklist.

Any hope of continuing in that way in blissful ignorance ended when her mother called demanding to know where Laila had disappeared to for months on end with "her precious grandsons" in tow. Which was laughable because Mama only visited once in six months, given her "busy career," and had only missed Laila when she'd needed petty cash or when she needed to be looked after by the daughter she knew worked damned hard.

She'd had no choice but to tell her that she was with the Skalas family—yes, *that* Skalas family—because Sebastian Skalas was Nikos and Zayn's father. Too late she had added it was not a good time to visit but it was lost in the furor Mama created at the identity of the boys' father.

She'd resigned herself to paying the price of keeping that explosive information to herself for more than two years in the form of unlimited amount of criticism in the future. She definitely didn't want them to come here and…somehow undercut Laila in an already overwhelming situation. But, of course, the model of chaos had always ruled her life. Why shouldn't it now?

They arrived one gray, drizzly evening, leaving her feeling as rootless and ignored as she always felt around them.

As it had been through her entire childhood and adolescence, Mama and Nadia's arrival caused quite the stir. Not just because they were two extremely beautiful women dressed to the height of sophistication, but because Mama had been a world-renowned actress in the '90s and Nadia was a supermodel, albeit one whose career had barely touched superstardom before spiraling down because she had the worst kind of work ethic. Also, there was not even a hint of resemblance between Laila and them.

She could see the surprise in everyone, probably wondering how Laila could be part of a family of women who looked like *that*. It was like she'd reverted back to being fifteen and gawky and awkward, her brain far too ahead of her body, wondering what she could do to look like them, how she could transform herself so that she belonged to that nest.

Before her adolescent nightmares could become truly fresh, her sensitive child came to her rescue in his own way. Reacting to Mama's frenetic, frantic energy, Zayn made his way to her, and wrapped his chubby arms around Laila's legs, begging wordlessly for respite.

Laila picked him up, hugging his small body to hers, feeling that sense of peace fall into place, like it always did when she held one of her sons. As long as she had her boys, she needed nothing. It had been her mantra since she'd held them both moments after they were born but now, as she observed Sebastian's smiling reception of her family, that conviction that she didn't need a man in her life stumbled and stuttered.

And even now, it wasn't that she needed Sebastian so much as she wanted him to need her. To want to spend the rest of his life with her. To choose it because he couldn't bear it otherwise. Apparently, her heart was just as romantic and delusional as her half sister, who kept throwing herself at men who didn't value her for anything but her beauty. But she didn't want to walk away from him, either.

Could she live in this weird limbo, then? Could she bear to marry him and live with the little he would give her while her love and her doubts niggled away at her? Would she ever feel confident enough to even admit to him without some guarantee of return?

No, a voice retorted.

She'd never been able to tell Mama that she craved her attention and her affection, or to Nadia that her taunts hurt, that she wanted to be part of them even if she was different. Or even Baba that she was only a teenager who still needed his care, even after Mama broke his heart.

God, she was a coward.

She gritted her teeth, as if to brace herself against the unbidden thoughts. Zayn cried out at the sudden stiffness of her hold, and she forced herself to relax her arms, cooing wordlessly into his temple, muttering *sorry.*

Sebastian was at her side instantly, his brow furrowed, as he tried to not crowd Zayn. "Laila, are you—"

"I'm fine," she said, without meeting Sebastian's eyes.

He moved closer, his broad frame shielding her from the prying eyes. "You're not happy to see them," he said, a thread of dismay in his statement.

She pursed her lips, unable to force even a parody of smile. "They are just a…lot."

"I will send them away, then," he said, rubbing his

finger over her chin, in an almost tentative gesture that raised her shocked gaze to him. As if he thought she might…push him away.

"No," she said, looking into his deep gray gaze and swallowing. God, the drama that would cause… She needed to stop being a coward. "They are family. And family is everything, isn't it?" she whispered.

He searched her gaze for a few moments, and then turned. His welcome words to Mama and Nadia told her he was *that* Sebastian again, the one she didn't want. She gingerly brought Zayn down to the floor, who instantly ran off to play with Annika, right as she was engulfed in her mother's perfume and her sister's air kisses.

Mama thanked Sebastian with the effusiveness that seemed to grow out of proportion for a man who'd simply slept with Laila—or in proportion with the Skalas name, for his gracious invitation to the villa Skalas, when her own daughter had conveniently omitted them from her good news.

Sebastian *had* invited them here, then. That explained his dismay.

Why, though?

"Laila has been looking lost these last few weeks. I thought seeing her family might help. And I was eager to meet her family," Sebastian replied, ever the charmer, though his gaze sought hers.

Pasting a smile to her lips, Laila looked away. For the first time since she had arrived at the villa, she wished the Skalas family wasn't all present in force. But, of course, they were curious to meet her family and clearly shocked at what she'd hidden.

She introduced Sebastian to Nadia, who demanded it with that usual diva flourish of hers, and wondered if her retinas could be damaged in the face of the radiant smile Nadia threw at Sebastian. She could sense her sister's growing interest as clearly as she could hear her own thudding pulse. Nadia shook his hand, asked after a common acquaintance and had him pealing in laughter within seconds. Nadia, who knew all about art, and high culture and fashion and business and celebrity… everything about the world Sebastian dwelled in and Laila knew nothing about, nor was interested in.

God, what was wrong with her? She'd never been jealous of her sister even as a pimply, gawky teenager. All she'd ever wanted was not to be so different from them, to belong. She wasn't going to do this to herself now, just because she was in love with him. Although, saying that to herself didn't take away sticky, ugly jealousy that consumed her.

"This is quite the pairing, no? Like a comical, reverse retelling of a particular fairy tale," Nadia said, guffawing at her own cheap joke that couldn't quite hide her upset at her sister's sudden bout of good fortune, both in looks and riches of the man she'd "*landed*." Her half sister had never quite learned to hide her pettiness. "The charming, gorgeous playboy Sebastian Skalas…"

A full-body cringe took hold of Laila as her meaning sunk. Embarrassment choked her throat as she whispered, "Nadia…"

"And our clever little numbers freak Laila Jaafri. If I didn't know your chances of succeeding were quite low and that you know next to nothing about seduction, I would've said you targeted him on purpose, Laila." She added a tinkling laugh as if to take the sting out of the words, which had never really worked and didn't now. "I mean, how else would you have met a man like him?"

Laila froze, no response rising to her lips. The hurried exit of Nikos and Zayn from the room with the ever-watchful Paloma at that exact moment meant everyone heard Nadia's comment, and her incapability to offer a token protest made it land like truth usually did—with unassailable certainty.

Alexandros and Thea stiffened. Even Annika's gaze widened as it found hers. She'd never told even her friend how she and Sebastian had met. For a weak, vulnerable moment, Laila found herself hoping Sebastian would come to her rescue.

"Oh, my God, you did target him," Nadia said with genuine shock, then considered Laila with a calculating glint.

"Fine, I did. But not for the horrible reason I see in your eyes. Not for his wealth, or his power or his…good looks," Laila bit out through gritted teeth, having had enough. Not for her sister's or Mama's sake or for her new family's sake. For her own sake. "I did it to protect Guido. Because Sebastian was…"

"Guido?" Mama and Alexandros said at the same time. His gaze swung to Sebastian and something dawned in his eyes.

"What does this have to do with that useless old goat?" Mama demanded.

Laila's gaze inexorably went to Sebastian's, even as

she automatically, like a thousand times before, said to her mother, "Guido is family to me. Mama."

"You don't have to cover up my sins, *pethi mou*," Sebastian said, holding her gaze from across the room, his words smooth and yet, somehow to her ears, full of tension. "Or protect me from the world."

He chuckled and it sounded so…so broken that Laila wanted to banish the entire world and go to him.

"*I* promised to protect you, not the other way around. Though, it is clear, I failed at that, too," he said, casting a glance at her family.

But Laila was loath to speak of what he had done, loath to betray what belonged to them to the whole damned world. Suddenly, she was glad of his mask in front of her family, even with his own, and most of the world. Because the real Sebastian, he was hers. His sins and his wounds and his real laughter, they were all hers and she would not share him with anyone. "How we met is no one's business," she finally said,

"Did you get pregnant on purpose, too?" Nadia asked, as if she'd rehearsed her lines. "That's quite the diabolical—"

"That's enough, Nadia," Laila said, disgust more than anger coming to her aid. How had she always let Nadia get away with this? Why had she tried to maintain a relationship that was all work on her part and insults on her sister's?

"Behave yourself, Nadia," Mama broke in, always a little late with her warning and little too indulgent of her eldest's disgraceful behavior. "It is of no consequence how it happened. The boys belong to this family and that's that."

No one could miss the satisfaction in her voice at that statement. Before Laila could interrupt, her mother continued, "Imagine our shock when Laila told us where she and the boys were, and with whom," Mama said to fill the awkward silence, waving her manicured hands about in that way of hers, looking elegant in a blush pink cream pantsuit that draped perfectly over her tall, statuesque figure. "Three years, she hid the identity of the father. Only that… Guido knew."

Out of the periphery of her vision, Laila saw Sebastian's head jerk up at that.

"You never asked me," Laila said.

"Of course I did. Many, many times," Mama said, making a liar out of Laila. "And honestly, I don't understand why you were so adamant about doing it all by yourself when you could have had this from the beginning. It's that middle-class mentality you inherited from your father."

"If wanting to stand on my own two feet, and wanting to have control over my life is middle class, then so be it. And please, don't bring Baba into this."

Mama turned to face Sebastian, a shrewd glint in her eyes, as if Laila hadn't even spoken. "I hope you're making financial settlements for my grandsons, Mr. Skalas. They deserve a cut of all this."

Laila's gaze found the floor, wishing it would open up and swallow her whole.

"Of course, Mrs. Syed," Sebastian replied as if it weren't the crassest question he had ever had to face.

"And make arrangements to clear Laila's debts, too, I hope? My daughter has quite the clever brain for numbers and patterns and models but none when it comes to finances. She has a mountain of debts because she insists on keeping her father's old house with its massive archives instead of—"

"That's enough, Mama," Laila said, a lifetime's worth of ache and anger bursting through. As much as Mama and Nadia had had very little actual time for Nikos and Zayn, she had tried. God, she had tried so hard to make them a part of her life because her sons deserved to know their grandmother and their aunt. But not at the cost of hearing them belittle their mother.

It had been stupid of her to think anything would change, after all these years. She was the one who had to change, the one who had to find the courage to let go of foolish hopes. Even if it hurt.

Her mother looked as if Laila had struck her.

"Don't take that tone with me, Laila."

"If it's the only one you'll hear, I have no choice." She tilted her chin up and addressed them both. "You didn't come to see the boys until they were three months old. You criticize everything I do as a parent. All my life, you've never spoken one loving word to me, and you drove Baba to his death with your constant demands and criticism. And now you stand there, revealing our family's secrets, without even checking how

I'm doing. You talk about Baba's research of a lifetime as some dirty secret you can't wait to throw into the garbage. I'm so done with you." She pulled in a big breath even as her throat felt like it was full of thorns. "Sebastian has no duty toward clearing our family's debts—most of which you and Nadia accrued by living far above your means. I'll not take a single euro from him or his family and neither of you will you get your hands on anything unless you plan to…rob your own grandsons blind."

"You have changed," Nadia said softly, angry splotches on her impossibly high cheeks, as if she was discovering only now that Laila wasn't kidding. Laila felt her gaze on her body like some kind of laser pointer searching for a weak spot. And right now, she felt like she was covered in holes and wounds she'd rather bare in front of a predator than her sister. "Maybe because you think you have all this?"

"Enough, Nadia," Laila said, tears prickling behind her eyes as they always did when she fought with her sister, when she realized all her childhood dreams of belonging to a loving family would remain just that. God, but not anymore. She had people who respected her, liked her, she had someone like Sebastian in her corner, and that filled her with the courage she'd always lacked. "Having all this, for me, means knowing that I don't have to worry about food and shelter and education for Nikos and Zayn. Your debts and Mama's debts would've ruined their lives. And yes, I get to wear a few new clothes and a fancy hairstyle and new makeup bought with his money. So what if I get to enjoy a few nice expensive things that have never been within my reach because you and Mama leached every last little bit out of Baba? I find no shame in accepting what Sebastian spends on me when it brings him pleasure. I find no shame in depending on him when he wants the best for our family."

"You're nothing but his sons' mother, Laila. Don't go pinning all your hopes on him," Nadia mock whispered, making sure everyone heard her.

Laila turned away. Why was it so much worse to hear your own worst fears in someone else's words? "You need to leave."

"Sebastian would marry her today if she agreed," Annika said, from across the room, forever riding to Laila's rescue, her dear, lovely friend.

Sebastian straightened from across the room and Laila shook her head to warn him off. She could see a vein ticking away in his jaw, the violent emotions swirling beneath the calm gray. This…ugly showdown with her family was long due and she had to be the one to do it.

Laila could see Nadia's shock, her mother's excitement before her sister reverted to her default setting of petty cruelty. "But you haven't accepted, have you?" Each step Nadia took toward her resonated with her heart's thud-thud. "Our dear Laila always has high standards. But that's not it this time, huh? Even you, with your head buried in numbers, must know what a prize you have landed."

"He's a man, not cattle," Laila said through gritted teeth.

"You will ruin this good fortune, just like your papa and…no, this is something else…" Nadia's stunning brown eyes widened. "You're in love with him." A tinkling laugh followed her declaration. "Oh…poor Laila. Of course you have fallen in love. But you should know that a man like that is never going to love you."

That soft gray gaze found hers in the sea of embarrassment and pain threatening to drown her and Laila didn't flinch or look away this time. She held Sebastian's gaze, marveling at the emotion beating in her chest as if it were a life unto itself, and tilted her chin up.

She would not shy away from him, now. But for once, she could not read him, either, as if he had pulled a curtain down to shut her out, too.

For all the shame she had felt all her life that she was different, all the shame she'd been made to feel by two women who should have loved her and protected her, for all the shame she'd felt that Sebastian would see how little she mattered to her own family, Nadia's petty declaration in front of everyone didn't cause that prickly emotion.

There was no shame in the fact that she had fallen in love with Sebastian. No wrong, no naïveté, no foolishness and definitely no logic to it.

But she only felt strong in her love, changed by meeting this man who had worked so hard to hold on to his true self, despite everything he'd faced as a child, no less. She'd been fortunate enough to know and love her father, to know and adore Guido, and now she was glad she had met Sebastian, even if it was through nefarious means, that she had borne his sons. That she would always love him for all the freedom he had pushed her to enjoy, whatever the future held for him.

The ache of not knowing how he felt would come soon enough, but for now, loving him was a strength holding her up.

She'd always been naive when it came to her mother and sister, forever hoping that they would change, but she wasn't stupid. And wherever she and Sebastian fell in the scheme of things, she had enough faith in him that he would always stand with her and their sons, against the entire damned world if needed.

Laila straightened her shoulders, wondering if that little spark of fire within her that was her love had changed how she looked, too. She poked her finger into Nadia's bony chest hard enough that her sister startled. "You aren't even clever enough to get on my good side knowing I could help you this time, no? Get out of my life, Nadia, and please, stay gone. Next time you decide to pay a visit, I'll have Annika call the police on you. Believe me, she's bloodthirsty enough to take you on even if I weaken."

Then she looked at her mother, who appeared pale and wan under her tan skin. Maybe finally realizing the magnitude of her errors. *Or not.*

"If you want to be a part of your grandsons' life, come back without her. And ask for my forgiveness. Then, maybe, I'll consider it, only because Baba taught me that love is more important than anything else."

Laila didn't wait to see how her words landed. Her throat burned like it had when she'd had the flu and she could barely swallow past the hurt sitting there. But at least, it was done.

CHAPTER TWELVE

It was dawn the next morning when Laila wrapped a flimsy cashmere sweater around her shoulders and knocked hard on the door to Sebastian's painting cabin or whatever the hell he chose to call it. Cold burned her skin but she didn't care. When he'd have followed her, she'd begged him to get rid of her mother and sister.

Then she had spent most of the night awake, crying on and off, which had predictably set off Zayn and then it was hours to calm him down and then waiting for Sebastian to come find her and then walking through the damned villa looking for him like some nighttime wraith.

She had been feeling raw after that confrontation with her mother and sister. Then, to realize that Sebastian wasn't coming… All her hope and pain turned to blazing anger, fueled by his…indifference to her plight, which he had brought on. And then there was the elephant in between them he was clearly, simply going to ignore.

As if her love would just fizzle out like Nikos's cold or Zayn's bad temper.

She had to thump hard a few more times before the double doors opened with a clunk, and there he was, on the other side of the threshold, looking as if he was the one who had been through a toxic breakup with his family. She didn't wait for him to welcome her inside. Neither did she politely wait for him inside the front lobby or whatever it was.

Pushing past him, she forced herself through the open door and into what was clearly an architectural marvel of a space, because it was all glass walls and high glass ceilings and dawn was like fingers painting the horizon pink and orange.

Once her attention returned to the room itself, she could see a huge number of paintings covered with plastic sheets and a fair number, also half-covered, sitting on easels, spread around the vast room. For a second, she indulged in the idea of unveiling each one with a dramatic flourish and taking a peek. But she had once violated his privacy out of necessity. Now that she knew it was something more than just his privacy, she was loath to do it again, however angry she was with him.

Her anger was already losing steam, and when she turned around to face him, it was to see a bleakness in his eyes that she never wanted to see again. The absence of that easy smile, or the charming mask or even the more real grumpy mood he'd shown her these past few weeks, made her skin prickly with a sense of caution. But it was too late, for she was realizing the freedom to be found in truth.

She wondered if she was getting her wish, finally, if she was seeing the raw, burning center of him, and she wondered belatedly, if that meant that she was going to burn with him. But there was not a speck of fear within her.

"I knew you were manipulating me to a certain extent. I knew you only wanted me because you want Nikos and Zayn in your life but I never thought you would be a coward, Sebastian."

He said nothing. Because, of course, Sebastian Skalas the charming playboy, never lied. He only just twisted the truth enough to make it palatable, for whoever he was serving it to. She had fallen in love with him with all this information at her fingertips, and yet now she felt a strange desolation. "You invited my family here and then, it felt like…why?"

"Alexandros had an extensive background check done on your friends and family recently. He was surprised when he found out who they were, who you were."

"Wow, infringing on privacy much?" she said, wondering even now at how he didn't ask why she hadn't told him. Why she'd kept her infamous family a secret.

"I didn't look, Laila, because it didn't make a difference to me. He mentioned your father was a minor prince."

"The title was mostly honorary at this stage. He had lands, but he sold off parcel by parcel to keep Mama happy. He was a good man but an idealist. He never had a job, and he buried himself in his research of his family's art history, which was his true passion, invested the little we had unwisely because her demands were endless, and lost it all. Then when it became clear that she had left him behind, he shut himself in the flat I rented for months at a time and wasted away to nothing.

I couldn't…save him. And I couldn't bear to go into that flat after. All his research, it's all sitting there."

"And you looked after him. And Guido and Paloma and your mother and Nadia."

She shrugged, not even a little surprised at his conclusion. It was a little unnerving but also liberating how clearly he saw her.

She had done that most of her life, she realized now—looked after people. She looked after Baba, at the end, when he'd been heartbroken that he couldn't keep up with her mother's constant demands, and buried himself in his archives and in his research. She'd made him meals, made him coffee, reminded him of his medication for his heart trouble. Then she had looked after Guido and Paloma, who had been dependent on her for their livelihood. She looked after Mama every time she got sick and came home because she was an awful patient and, of course, Nadia couldn't be trusted to even bring her a glass of water. She had looked after even Nadia when she would come home after another one of her spectacular breakups with men who were as shallow as she was, hoping that she and her sister would maybe form a new bond.

When Guido had told her what he'd gambled away, she'd taken care of that, too.

The only person who had ever looked after her was Sebastian, albeit with a goal in mind, but hadn't his care for her come from some other place later?

If she agreed to marry him now—knowing he would devote himself to her and the boys, knowing that belonging to him meant she would never be alone again—

would she be happy? Or would she forever wonder about what he truly felt for her? Would she forever trap herself in that toxic place again like she'd done with Mama and Nadia?

What did she reach for? The known, stable contentedness or risk it all for his love?

She rubbed a hand over her gritty-feeling eyes. "Why did you invite them?"

"We were at an impasse. Something happened the last time you were here," he said, spreading his arms to span the cabin. "My goal to convince you to marry me seemed further away than where I'd started. I thought bringing your family here would be a good thing. I thought I could score another point off with you. I didn't realize how awful they are to you." He laughed but it carried no real humor. "Alexandros thought it was important to control the situation since they are in the public eye, too."

She laughed then. But it was not bitter, and she was glad because she did not want to become like her mother, who lived in ideals that had nothing to do with reality, or her father, who had given his heart to an undeserving woman and died of it being broken. "I should've known it's all a game to you."

He shook his head, frustration coloring his words. "You seemed…sad the last couple of weeks, as if you were retreating inward, going somewhere I could not…follow."

"You know why now, Sebastian," she said, throwing the gauntlet back down again. But when he let it writhe in the space between them, she tried to gather her armor back. "I guess it did turn out to be the right thing for me. That confrontation has been coming a long time and I wouldn't have done it, if not for the last three months, if not for knowing that I have you in my corner."

"You were glorious, Laila. You did what you had to do."

"I always wanted to be like them," she said, only now realizing how much it hurt to give up on those you loved.

"You're a million times more beautiful than either of them," Sebastian said, as if he could see through her to that little girl she'd been.

"You know what?" she said, seeing herself clearly for the first time in a long time. Seeing herself through his gaze helped, too, because he'd always wanted her. That much had always been real between them. "I think I'll believe you."

"I also understand how much what I did to Guido hurt you."

"After Baba passed away, he was the one who watched out for me. He…never abandoned me."

"And you didn't abandon yourself, *ne*?"

"No, I didn't. Even when it was hard. You see all this, Sebastian, and yet you withdraw here and wonder why I would fall in love with you?"

"Laila—"

"What? That wasn't part of the plan? Is it an inconvenient plot twist to the narrative you had mapped out in your head about how this would go?"

She looked like a fury he had once painted, rising out of the mountains, all stark, raw beauty and righteous anger with the gentlest spirit beneath if only one was brave enough and vulnerable enough to seek it. He had drawn it after Mama had left. He hadn't known it then, but he had drawn what he wished she could have been for him and Alexandros.

And finally, here was the woman he'd imagined once, in blood and flesh, taunting him to come closer, boldly declaring her love.

Hair flying in all directions, eyelids swollen and amber eyes red-rimmed, that wide bow-shaped mouth pinched, her frame swathed in his T-shirt, crackling with temper, threatening ruin and yet, promising salvation if only he went to his knees and surrendered.

Sebastian, as he usually did when he finished a huge piece like that, felt inadequate, small, torn apart, feeling none of the succor he thought he would have once he finished. He felt like that child again, wondering what he'd done to deserve this fate and wishing he could change it, even though it was the dream he'd once held closest to his heart.

He had set out to win Laila over to his way. He'd even found her naive and easy in one sense because she was so…fair and logical to begin with. She wanted nothing but their sons' happiness and honest desire between them. She just wanted a place for herself and he'd been happy to give it. But he'd never dreamed of her…falling in love with him, much less declaring it like this, or coming up with a fresh set of demands.

Even saying that made him want to roar and howl in a way he hadn't done since he had been a teenager who had constantly wished he was like his brother.

It had taken all his willpower to let her sister take strips off Laila right in front of him. And then that taunt and Laila's silence in the wake of it.

The bold, brave way she'd held his gaze.

He still didn't know what to make of it. Only that it terrified him to his soul, that he felt…that same sense of powerlessness he'd felt as a kid with his father in the face of her love. Like he didn't deserve it and didn't know what to do with it.

He thrust a hand through his hair. "I don't know what you want from me."

She smiled, and it was fragile and heartbreakingly beautiful. "Why were you so determined to ruin Guido?" she said, surprising him yet again. "Please, I deserve to know. I demand to know."

And he knew that she was hacking away at all the shields he hid behind, tearing away all the blinders and smokescreens he used to keep the world at bay. She was going to bring him to his knees if he wasn't there already and there was nothing he could do to stop her.

"He used to be Mama's chauffeur. One summer, he helped her run away without raising Konstantin's doubts one bit. I wanted to know where she went."

"After all these years?" she said, tears in her eyes.

"I have never stopped wanting to make sure she was okay," he said with a shrug. Not that he had understood that compulsion, either. Like with everything else about his head, he had simply given in. At some point, it had become less about any attachment he'd still felt for Mama and more a reason to continue in the aimless way he'd adapted his life to be.

"But Guido wouldn't tell you?"

"No. Not even when I had the deed to his small house in my control."

"And now? Do you still want to find her?"

He blew out a breath. "I will not say no. But the choke hold has lessened. Alexandros told me recently that she had planned to take me with her when she fled. That she'd packed my passport and my medication in her little bag, that somehow Konstantin might have upset her plan at the last minute, and she had to flee instantly."

"And leave Alexandros behind to your father? Rip you, too, from him? That's extraordinarily cruel," she said, and he could see the rage she was working hard to temper.

"I agree," he said, remembering the bleakness in his twin's face when he had revealed that piece of the past that had tormented him for so long. "I think he thought it would bring me solace after all these years to know that she wanted me with her. I was more attached to her from the beginning and… I wouldn't stop looking for her."

"But it didn't work out like Alexandros thought it would," she said, so damned perceptive.

"Other than ripping him apart for God knows how long with guilt that he'd hidden it from me, no."

"Did you tell him that you would have never abandoned him?"

It felt like the punches kept coming, like he was already on his knees, but she wouldn't leave him until he was bloody and broken. "So sure of me, Laila?"

"I know you, Sebastian. Better than anyone else in the world. Maybe even better than Alexandros."

That piece of truth moved through him like a bullet, ricocheting through the chambers of his chest. And he was beginning to understand why he felt hunted. "I did tell him that I'd have never left him. And in the end, Mama chose her freedom over me, too. I never blamed her for being weak in the face of Konstantin's will."

One lone tear followed the strong cheek down to her chin. Strangely, her tears on his behalf didn't bother Sebastian one bit. Because she understood exactly how he felt? Because she could see who he was beyond all that he had endured?

He felt a cold chill and a hot flare at the very pit of his being. It was the freedom he'd chased all his life—to be seen as he was—and yet denied himself because he'd been determined to be far from the shadow of the past. He'd bound himself in the shackles of the Skalas name as much as Alexandros had done, just in a different way. He hadn't outrun the name at all.

He had almost lost the chance to know about his sons. And now, when he had them within reach, within his home, within his heart, it was not enough. The means had become the end…and suddenly, Sebastian Skalas, one of the most renowned, brilliant artists of their time, a near mythical man who could alchemize emotion into colors, who could pin down the world into one blank canvas in all its glory and its disgrace, didn't know if he was enough. If he could withstand the love of this woman, if he could stand under its shadow and not freeze to ice, if he could ever…return it without conditions and contracts and…the crippling fear that he would lose it all. That something within him—some rot that his father had planted—wouldn't push her away.

"After seeing you with the boys…" he continued, determined to get it all out, because she was hollowing him out anyway, "I knew Alexandros was not wrong in being angry with Mama all these years, in blaming her as much as he did Konstantin for our ruined childhoods. A few hours after that first night, I knew how it could be. How it should be."

She took a grasping, watery breath as if she were the one living through the past.

"And yet, you're here," she said, walking toward him, "making glorious art and loving your sons right from the first minute and being a man in your own right, and being this extraordinarily kind man. I…" She smiled weakly through the tears and straightened her shoulders. "I know what I want for my third wish."

He barked a laugh out then and he thought it might be the little bit of sanity he'd hung on to all these years leaving his system, rendering him into the stark skeleton of the child he'd been born, with dreams and demons all occupying the same space within his head, able to see the world for what it was and for once, loving it the same anyway.

For all he'd blamed Konstantin as the reason, he'd been running away from life, directionless. Running away from the very spirit of the child he'd been, who'd loved endlessly and lived fearlessly.

"What would you have of me, *agapi mou*?" he said, finally beaten down and admitting defeat. All the battles he'd fought in his life, and he hadn't even seen this one coming.

She reached him and clasped his unshaven cheeks and pulled him down to meet her mouth and it was heaven and hell and the purgatory he'd existed in for so long. It was unbearable pleasure with a twist of pain in its promise. Her mouth was soft, and so incredibly sweet and he was a dying man parched of breath itself. Small hands gripped his shoulders as if she meant to anchor him to her in any way possible. He felt drenched to his soul in the affection of her kiss, in the passion of her response, drowned in her unnamed expectations. But weak man that he was, he couldn't push her away.

She touched her forehead to his, rubbed her nose against his like she did with their sons and smiled against his mouth. Her tears only reminded him of his unending thirst. "I want to marry you, Sebastian. I want to build a life with you. I want to share your art and celebrate your ups and downs. I want to have more children with you. I want to love you for the rest of our lives, and I want it more than anything I've ever wanted in this world. And I want it with you loving me, as only you can."

"Then you might have to wait a long time, Dr. Jaafri," he said, his heart breaking, even as it felt out of his reach. A paradox if he'd seen one and he had seen enough in his life.

"I have time. You should know, patience is one of my virtues, too. I have made all the calculations here—" she tapped her head "—and here—" then her chest "—and it all adds up. My life is here with you and our sons."

"I could grant you a thousand wishes, a million and make them all true. Whatever you ask for. Except this. Don't—"

"I know what I want, and I won't settle for anything less," she said, walking away from him.

At the door, she stilled and turned around. "Remember the academic paper I submitted?"

He nodded, feeling as if he were in a trance.

"It got accepted. I get to present it at a conference in a couple of weeks in London. I'm planning to go away and leave the boys here with you."

"Zayn—"

"Zayn trusts you and loves you, Sebastian. He just needs the push to come to you and without me here acting as a security blanket, it will happen seamlessly. You trust me, don't you?"

If he didn't know her well, he'd have thought she was flexing her newfound confidence and the strength of her hold on him. But he did know her, and he was also aware that her love would haunt him for the rest of his life, reminding him of his fear. He nodded, refusing to give her the words, resentful of the understanding shining in her eyes.

"Paloma will be here just in case."

"Why two weeks?" he asked, though a part of him felt relief that she was going away. That he didn't have to face those amber eyes and the unfathomable trust in them, in the mornings, in the afternoons and during midnights when they checked on their sons. The coward in him wished she'd go away for longer, even, wished he could return to whom he had been before she'd walked into his life, blasting open every defense he'd put up against the world.

But there was also that part that hated the thought of her being out in the world without him. With colleagues and friends and some man who might see what an extraordinary woman she was. He felt torn in two and it was more painful than anything he'd ever experienced.

"I hung on to my father's flat for too long, as a way of keeping him with me. I never stepped foot inside those walls again. But now, I want to sort through his research before Mama decides she will burn it all. I want to do something with it. I want to save it so that our sons can learn about their legacy on my side, too."

"I can arrange for someone to—"

"No. I must do this. Say goodbye properly. Tell him I'm starting a new chapter in my life. And that he's given me everything I needed to thrive, that he was right when he told me that I'm worth everything the world has to offer, just as I am."

"I would have loved to meet him."

She nodded, smiling. "He would have loved to meet you, too. And he would have liked you."

Already he could feel her absence, the one person he'd ever allowed into this space.

"If I'm never ready to grant you your wish?" he whispered, feeling as if he was being attacked from all sides, swept away by a tide he couldn't fight. "If we're forever caught in this…limbo?"

"Never is a long time, Sebastian. As for the limbo, I guess we can both survive in a way, for our sons, remain stagnant and static, instead of choosing something more. But I can't…" She swallowed, her eyes searching his. "…marry you unless you—"

"It doesn't happen because you threaten or beg or demand it. Believe me, I have tried."

"No but it won't happen if you close yourself to it, either. And I want you to give us a chance, to crack open the door, to let me in. You've been hiding in shadows and secrets long enough."

And then she was gone, and Sebastian wished the coming dawn would stop and leave him in darkness for a long time because after everything, it seemed Konstantin's shadow had won and he had lost.

Because the thought of loving Laila, the thought of opening himself to her love, felt terrifying to his very soul.

CHAPTER THIRTEEN

SEBASTIAN LOOKED UP at the tiny third-floor flat in the small coastal village, where he'd been sitting in the car for the last two hours. With the windows rolled down and a storm front coming in, he was freezing.

And he had frozen ever since he'd arrived here, with a note clutched in his hand, disappearing like a coward the moment he knew she was back.

For almost two months now, Laila and he had been engaged in a silent battle of wills when they were in each other's company. Which had been less than usual since she'd traveled out of country three separate times. With him deep in finishing a few pieces for his next exhibit and Laila traveling back and forth for work and to clear out her father's house while doing her best to preserve his research, they had crossed each other at the villa no more than for a handful of days.

And he was beginning to hate everything about their life, enmeshed together but not intersecting in any but the shallowest of ways. She didn't smile at him or argue with him or probe him or touch him. She just looked at him with that steady, relentless emotion in her eyes, whether they were playing with their sons or discussing her career or sleep-mussed from his bed, which she had taken over and he didn't mind.

Sebastian found himself shrinking, to escape seeing himself through her eyes.

His brother and Ani were baffled by the silent but pregnant stalemate between them. Even his sons, he knew, were beginning to feel the rift between him and Laila and he found himself bereft, on the verge of losing everything he'd gotten a taste of in the past weeks.

His fear of letting her in was nothing compared with the torment of seeing her in his bed and not reaching for her. Of wanting to hear those sweet words from her lips again and depriving himself because he wasn't sure he could pay the price.

Then he'd seen it, a handwritten note with two lines of address on it, left on his desk. And he'd known instantly that it was from Laila, known that she'd scoured through her father's research and Guido's belongings for this. She'd been gone to find this.

For him.

Because she wanted Sebastian to have what he'd looked for most of his life.

But now that he was here, now that Sebastian knew that his mother was in that third-floor flat, all he felt was a strange relief. A freedom. Like he was ready to set down the weight of whatever had been clinging to him.

Laila had gotten him what he'd wanted and that, too, like her love, felt like an unbinding. A releasing. A new beginning for him. For them. For their sons and their lives together.

When he heard a noise from the tiny balcony, Sebastian froze. He could hear the litany of Greek, was almost sure that it was *her*. But he didn't need to go up and confront her. He didn't need to check if she was okay. He didn't need to ask her how she could have abandoned him and Alexandros.

He didn't need any answers from her, not anymore. Not when he had an entire life waiting for him. Not when everything he had ever sought was within him. Not when a woman like Laila could see what he was truly and still love him. The reason, the struggle, the culmination of all the battles he'd taken on in his life was in his house, waiting for him. Giving him what he had needed without him asking for it. Seeing him as he was.

So, he started the engine and he bid the woman on that balcony goodbye in his head and he drove off, even as he was still shaking from head to toe.

Laila felt strong arms gently pull Nikos from where he'd been clinging to her like an octopus but felt reluctant to open her eyes. She threw an arm behind her gently, only to find Zayn was gone, too.

Instantly, she turned and blinked, remembering she had carried both boys to her bed and fallen asleep, with their arms and legs wrapped all around her. On the rare occasions that she let them both come to bed, she was usually so stiff so as not to disturb their sleep. But tonight, she hadn't cared. She'd needed them, after two months of avoiding Sebastian's gaze, only to find that he wouldn't look at her at all. Then she'd been gone again with another goal in mind. And this time, she had known he would disappear. But still, it was hard because she wanted to be with him. Because she wanted to hold his hand when his world broke apart, all over again. Because she wanted to love him.

Not even Alexandros knew where his twin had gone off to and Laila kept it to herself. She had no intention of ruining the happiness that Alexandros had found with Annika by bringing up pieces of the past he'd finally made peace with. If Sebastian wanted to tell him, that was his choice.

In Sebastian's absence, his twin had taken to reassuring Laila that Sebastian was a good man, just…maybe a little broken. Even Thea seemed to think that Laila was just being both stubborn and foolish, playing this waiting game. Sebastian, she kept telling her, would never love her.

If his continued absence hadn't sowed doubts about the future—how long did it take to drive up to the coast and find that address?—Laila would have found the mighty Alexandros Skalas's nervous declarations a little funny. Neither did she agree with him or Thea at all.

She didn't think Sebastian was broken at all. Only a little bent like her, but somehow, they had both managed to retain the best of themselves and found people to love and they had their sons to nurture and…

The door to her vast bedroom that adjoined the boys' room was closed and footsteps returned to the bed.

She gasped when those very arms lifted her not-so-slender frame and shifted her to the middle of the bed. Instant tears pooled in her eyes when she realized it was *him*. He was cold and shaking behind her and she shivered at both. She felt his lips against the nape of her neck, cold and chapped. Alarm swept through her at what he'd been up to, what he had discovered at the address she'd found. "Sebastian? You're shivering. What happened? Is everything—"

"I want to hold you, Laila. I need to…"

She grabbed his corded forearm that gripped her tight under her breasts, smushing her front against his back so hard that her breath came in rough pants, compulsively running her fingers over the soft hair there, wanting to soothe him. His other hand, she brought to her face and kissed the center of his palm. "I missed you," she said, giving up all pretense of the fight she meant to put up when he returned. "I—"

"Shh…not right now, *agapi.* Right now, I need you. I need to feel your warmth and your passion and your need for me. Only you would provoke me to this, Laila. Only you could reduce me to this—"

"I'm yours, Sebastian. Take me. Have me. Do what you will with me. I have been yours from the first moment I saw you and you showed me a simple kindness I didn't know I needed. I had been yours three years ago. I have been yours all these months and I'll be yours fifty years from now, when you're not the stud you are now."

She felt his mouth stretch against her skin in a smile, felt it reach her deep within her being, that empty place waiting for him. She felt a shuddering relief that she hadn't lost him to the past, that she could make him smile, that she…

"I want to make you promises, give you what you deserve. But I—"

"It's okay, Sebastian. Right now, all I need is to be

what you need. My entire life, I have given so much of myself to people who didn't care. You… I would give you anything."

"I want you so much," he said, the tips of his fingers still cold as they dug into her willing flesh. "I'm afraid I might be rough…"

"I want you rough. And gentle. And all the speeds in between," she said, throwing her arm behind her in the dark and wrapping it around his neck.

When she turned her head, his mouth was there, ferociously demanding and desperately hungry. Just the way she needed him. His kiss was hot and hard and rough, his tongue stroking against her, his fingers on her chin holding her for his assault.

Laila moaned when his fingers snuck under her tank top and pinched her nipple. She pushed herself into him shamelessly, begging against his mouth for more. Protests fell from her tingling lips when he deserted her mouth, but his hands were all over her and she arched into his touch. For days, weeks, she'd been trying to nurture her hope, to fan it with tiny sparks that she felt living around his family, around his things, and yet it had only left her desolate. Cold.

Now, she was burning, and she wanted to go up in flames if it meant she could have him.

Soon, he'd pulled her top out of the way, baring her to him.

"I need to see you," came his ragged whisper, and then soft light from the lamp hit her closed eyes.

She kept them closed, too eager and loath to see his

expression, afraid that her own hopes might dash her to the ground all over again.

His breath was a feather-light whisper against her breasts, her nipples instantly tightening. Then she felt his tongue lash her nipple in slow, tentative strokes and then, when she buried her fingers in his hair and moaned, firm, fast circles that had her panting, and then his mouth sucked her in and he suckled deep and her eyes flew open.

Pupils blown so wide that she barely saw the gray, his mouth wet around her breast, he looked like her every fantasy come true. Dark circles clung to his eyes and his mouth had that pinched look, but all she saw was his hunger. For her. His need for her.

"More, Sebastian, please," she said, arching her spine into his warmth. "Don't make me wait anymore."

He rubbed his nose down her belly, whispering words into her skin, and then he stilled.

She looked down and saw him swallow at the sight of her wispy lace panties. "They're impractical and they ride up my ass half the time and I'm not used to them," she said, breathing hard. "But I wore them for you. In case you showed up. Every night, I take a shower, rub myself all over in some freaking expensive oil that comes with being *your woman* and dress in the flimsiest of clothes with the hope you'll come to me here and that you'll see me and that you'll admit that you love me a little."

His teeth pulled at the fragile lace before he kissed the line of her pelvis, rubbed his nose at the fold of her thigh and hip, digging his teeth into the sensitive skin of her inner thigh until she was marked in his ink. A sliver of pain to punctuate the pleasure. Laila curled her fingers in his hair and tugged roughly, just as he tore them off her, and then his mouth was there.

"You taste divine," he said, his words a rumble that caused vibrations against her folds. "I remember your taste. I remember how you sounded that night. I remembered how you looked at me."

"Please, Sebastian," she said, finding no shame in begging. "You made me wait too long already."

His fingers and his lips and his filthy whispers, he drove her hard and fast and rough and so high that Laila flew up and up and away and then she fell from that height, hard. Her climax was a vortex of sensation, thrashing her around and around. And he didn't stop tormenting her.

His tongue licked at her clit, his fingers kept pumping inside her until Laila went from one orgasm to the next with no break or breath in between and her entire body was nothing but a mass of sensation.

"I forgot how you can do that," he said, coming up and smiling, his sensuous lips damp with her arousal.

"Inside me, now," she said, the words barely formed. "I started the pill."

He swallowed and then that hard, lean, beautiful body was rising over her. His mouth found hers in a soft, tender kiss as if he knew she would break apart at the tiniest of pressures and his damp, hair-roughened chest dragged over her sensitive, throbbing nipples in a graze that sent need flickering into a spark again and then he was stretching her thighs indecently wide, pushing her right knee into her chest, and Laila watched him—his intense expression, his tied brows and his swollen lips and his unwavering focus—and then his gaze met hers.

He thrust into her in one smooth, deep move, lodging himself so deeply as he'd done that first time that she'd never been able to get him out. And now, she didn't want to.

She thrust her hips up and circled them, desperate for friction, and he cursed and swallowed.

And then he was moving in and out in a slow, deep rhythm, their fingers laced, and their gazes tethered together, and Laila's selfish mind and deprived body began the dance all over again.

"I'm going to take you fast and hard," he said, against her lips, and Laila whispered another *please*.

And then he upped their rhythm.

Each stroke hit that magical point, each thrust drove her further along the line of bliss, but Laila kept her eyes on him, this beautiful, rugged artist of hers, who felt so much and who tried so hard to not love her and she wanted to say the words now.

Clasping his cheek, she said, "I love you, Sebastian."

And as if he meant to reward her declaration, he took her deeper, dragging the ridge of his abdomen over her clit, and Laila fell over.

He pumped his hips, rough and fast, into her and then he was grunting and shaking and burying his face in her neck, and his weight on top of her, for the bare second he allowed it, was the most delicious pressure and Laila pressed her forehead to his shoulder and scrunched her eyes but her body betrayed her yet again and soon, there were tears running down her cheeks and dampening his taut skin in the process.

Sebastian stared helplessly at the softly snoring woman and didn't know what to make of the fact that Laila had not only sobbed as if her heart was breaking all over again, but then fallen into such deep sleep that he was terrified of waking her.

Gently untangling her limbs from his, he pressed a kiss to her temple, pulled on his sweatpants and quietly padded into their sons' bedroom.

Nikos was fast asleep, his toy horse clutched in his tiny fist.

"Papa?" he heard behind him.

Heart in his throat, he went to his second son, who'd pulled himself to his feet in the crib and had a hand outstretched toward him. While he hadn't run away from him or hid behind Paloma exactly when Laila had been gone, Zayn hadn't exactly sought Sebastian, either.

He was about to crouch down in front of him, wary of spooking him, when Zayn said, "Pick up, Papa. Want cuddle."

Tears knocking hard against his eyes, Sebastian sniffed and then picked up the little boy.

Tucking his little head into Sebastian's shoulder, arms thrown around his neck, Zayn didn't say much, and, in the silence, Sebastian's heart hammered out a thunderous beat.

He had no idea how long he walked around the vast bedroom, holding one piece of his jagged heart outside his body.

Two yawns and a softening of his body later, his son demanded "sleep now." Kissing his forehead, Sebastian was about to put him down on the bed when Zayn kissed his cheek. "Papa not go? Papa stay now?"

Tears crowding his throat, Sebastian said, "Yes, Zayn. Papa stay now. Papa's not going anywhere."

Zayn stared at him through sleep-heavy eyes and then two seconds later, fell into a deep sleep.

Sebastian walked between the two cribs a few times, and went off to shower, considering and discarding all the words he needed to say to the woman who'd given him more than he'd ever dreamed of.

When he returned to their bedroom in fresh pajamas hours later, with dawn cracking through the deepest dark of the night, his hair still wet, Laila was sitting up in the bed, the tank top back on, her legs folded under her, her head thrown back against the headboard of the bed. Her wide mouth was trembling, and she kept running a hand over her neck where he'd left a mark on her with his teeth, submerged in his climax.

He could sense her tension across the room as if it were his own and loathed that he had caused it. That he had made her doubt him. That he had made her wait.

She looked up just as he reached the bed. He stood there, watching her, arms hanging by his side uselessly, his heart beating so fast that it threatened to rip out of him.

"Zayn spoke to me, just now." His throat felt like it was full of needles and thorns. "He demanded a cuddle and demanded that I don't leave again."

"He missed you. He kept asking Nikos why you

left and when you were returning. For the first time, I saw them fighting because he wouldn't stop asking and Nikos got frustrated. It was both…exciting because they're growing such distinct personalities and terrifying because I never want them to lose each other."

"They won't," he said, feeling, for once, more confidence in their sons than she did. "Zayn… Did he get really upset?"

"A bit, yes. Like his papa, when he loves, he loves true and deep."

"Such faith, *agapi*?"

"It's both easy and hard, this whole loving-you thing. I… I feel like I'm perpetually on a roller coaster and you know I'm not fond of risks."

He sat at the edge of the bed and took her hand in his. "I…thank you for locating that address for me. I don't know what to think."

"Guido was exactly like Baba. He never threw away a single scrap of paper. Once I remembered that, it was easy. It took only four days and sleepless nights to find it neatly written in one of his address books. I think he meant to give it to me. He knew the boys were yours."

Sebastian nodded, brought her hand to his mouth and kissed her. All his life, words had come easily to him. Of comfort and teasing and charm and seduction and… yet now… He felt like his sons, his emotions too big and too fast for his throat to work.

"Did you see her? Is she well?" Laila asked softly, taking pity on him.

"I parked outside the flat and sat there for a few hours. I didn't feel the need to go in. Even after I heard her."

And then Laila was crawling into his lap, and he heaved them both onto the bed because there was no way he could let her fall. “I’m free, *agapi mou*. Finally. Thanks to you. Free of shadows and secrets. Free to love you. And I already do. I love you so much that I find words inadequate. I love you so much and I thank the entire universe every day, every moment that you decided to lie to me, and cheat me and seduce me and have our sons. I love your honesty and your calculations and your brainy brain and how you love our sons and how you fill my life with such happiness.”

Laila clung to him, her tears wetting her chest all over again, and Sebastian pushed her into the bed and stared into her amber eyes. “Tell me again.”

“I love you, Sebastian. Probably since I saw your art and how perceptive and stunning it was.”

“And will you marry me?”

“Yes. Tomorrow if you want.”

And then there was nothing to do but kiss her again and lose himself in her taste, and her groans and her sweet demands and her reverent promises.

EPILOGUE

LAILA AND SEBASTIAN'S SMALL, intimate wedding—which somehow still had a hundred guests because Thea Skalas was determined to have one grandson's wedding the way she wanted it—got postponed, since Nyra Skalas, their cutest, prettiest little niece, with a full head of thick dark hair and her mom's big brown eyes, decided to make an appearance way ahead of schedule, sending them all into a tailspin of shock and surprise and laughter and a small nervous breakdown on the part of her father, who had bellowed at his twin at the top of his lungs because Sebastian had mocked him.

Even though Ani and the newborn were doing well, Laila insisted on waiting because how could she get married without her new friend/sister acting as her maid of honor. But since Ani had to have a caesarean and Alexandros was like an enraged/terrified bull on steroids every time his wife or his twin or his grandmother dared to suggest that maybe, just maybe, Ani was ready to be up and about for such a big event, they pushed it back a little more.

Which, of course, made Sebastian angry because he thought his twin was overprotective and was the main obstacle in the way of what he'd waited for his whole life.

Laila, for her part, loved it all: Alexandros's utter love for his daughter, how Sebastian—a natural at this, too—showed him how to support his brand-spanking-new niece's tiny head, how Nikos and Zayn couldn't stop blubbering about their itty-bitty cousin, about the pictures Thea insisted they shoot on day three with her two great-grandsons and great-granddaughter, and how Alexandros had nearly broken into tears when Nyra had smiled at him even as Sebastian teased that it was aimed at him—the superior uncle—and how she and Ani had hugged and laughed and cried together knowing that they'd found the kind of love that very few did.

Finally, a month after Nyra was born, the day dawned bright and sunny and Laila followed Annika, who was holding Nyra in her arms, down the aisle on Alexandros's arm—she'd been stunned and awed when he'd asked to give her away—and there was Sebastian waiting for her, with Nikos and Zayn by his side, looking like his very heart was lodged into the look he gave her.

She cried and smudged her makeup and cried a little more when he kissed her and whispered, "Six months just for us and then we're making a baby and this time, I want a girl as precious as Nyra."

"It's not a competition, you know," she said, a while later, as he kissed the back of her hand and they were whizzing away in a chauffeured car for a quick two-day getaway because neither of them really wanted to leave Nikos and Zayn just yet to Paloma and Ani and Alexandros and Thea, even though everyone kept assuring them they would be fine.

"Of course it is. That way, we could keep the bigger chunk of the Skalas fortune for our children."

Leaning into him, she kissed his naughty mouth. "As if you would take anything away from the little girl you call your princess already."

He laughed and pulled her hand up, until the two rings there shone brightly. They were unique and tiny—despite his protestations—and just right for her. He kissed the back of her hand, his throat moving on a hard swallow.

"I love you, Mr. Skalas," she said, looking into his eyes.

"I love you more, Dr. Jaafri," he whispered, and then she was squealing because he was pulling her into his lap and kissing her senseless and Laila thought her dream had finally come true` with more color and love than she could have ever imagined.

* * * * *

If you couldn't get enough of this Tara Pammi story,
then make sure you catch up with
the first installment of
The Powerful Skalas Twins *duet*
Saying "I Do" to the Wrong Greek

And why not explore her previous books?

Returning for His Unknown Son
The Secret She Kept in Bollywood
Marriage Bargain with Her Brazilian Boss
The Reason for His Wife's Return
An Innocent's Deal with the Devil

Available now!